Rex Stout

REX STOUT, the creator [...] ille, Indiana, in 1886, the [...] and Lucetta Todhunter Sto[...] irth the family moved to W[...] in a country school, but l[...] zed throughout the state [...]. Mr. Stout briefly attended the University of Kansas, but he left to enlist in the Navy and spent the next two years as a warrant officer on board President Theodore Roosevelt's yacht. When he left the Navy in 1908, Rex Stout began to write freelance articles and worked as a sightseeing guide and an itinerant book-keeper. Later he devised and implemented a school banking system which was installed in four hundred cities and towns throughout the country. In 1927 Mr. Stout retired from the world of finance and, with the proceeds of his banking scheme, left for Paris to write serious fiction. He wrote three novels that received favorable reviews before turning to detective fiction. His first Nero Wolfe novel, *Fer-de-Lance*, appeared in 1934. It was followed by many others, among them, *Too Many Cooks*, *The Silent Speaker*, *If Death Ever Slept*, *The Doorbell Rang*, and *Please Pass the Guilt*, which established Nero Wolfe as a leading character on a par with Erle Stanley Gardner's famous protagonist, Perry Mason. During World War II Rex Stout waged a personal campaign against Nazism as chairman of the War Writers' Board, master of ceremonies of the radio program "Speaking of Liberty," and member of several national committees. After the war he turned his attention to mobilizing public opinion against the wartime use of thermonuclear devices, was an active leader in the Authors' Guild, and resumed writing his Nero Wolfe novels. Rex Stout died in 1975 at the age of eighty-eight. A month before his death he published his seventy-second Nero Wolfe mystery, *A Family Affair*. Ten years later, a seventy-third Nero Wolfe mystery was discovered and published in *Death Times Three*.

The Rex Stout Library

REX STOUT

Three Witnesses

Introduction
by Susan Conant

BANTAM BOOKS
NEW YORK · TORONTO · LONDON · SYDNEY · AUCKLAND

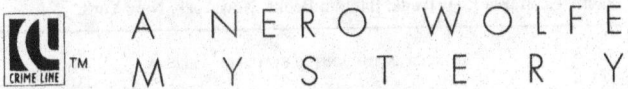

A NERO WOLFE MYSTERY

This edition contains the complete text
of the original hardcover edition.
NOT ONE WORD HAS BEEN OMITTED

THREE WITNESSES
A Bantam Crime Line Book / published by arrangement
with Viking Penguin

PUBLISHING HISTORY
Viking edition published March 1956
Bantam edition / July 1957
Bantam reissue edition / October 1994

CRIME LINE and the portrayal of a boxed "cl" are trademarks of Bantam
Books, a division of Random House, Inc.

ISBN 978-0-553-24959-0

Published simultaneously in the United States and Canada

Bantam Books are published by Bantam Books, a division of Random House,
Inc. Its trademark, consisting of the words "Bantam Books" and the portrayal
of a rooster, is Registered in U.S. Patent and Trademark Office and in other
countries. Marca Registrada. Bantam Books, New York, New York.

PRINTED IN THE UNITED STATES OF AMERICA

Introduction

When I was asked to introduce the novellas in this collection, I felt wary of the ominously titled "Die Like a Dog," which I had always imagined to be yet another better-left-unread mystery in which my favorite character, probably a German shepherd, would rapidly and gruesomely perish in some misguided foreshadowing of the so-called real murder. To reassure myself on the crucial quadrupedal point, I read the third of these novellas first. Delighted to discover that I could recommend it to even the most tender-hearted dog lover, I turned to the beginning of *Three Witnesses* only to find myself assailed by self-doubt. In every Rex Stout I had ever read, Archie Goodwin had ably performed the introductions with no help from me. I was thus relieved to discover that, despite their doglessness, the first two novellas in *Three Witnesses* required a few introductory remarks that I was, after all, qualified to make.

"The Next Witness" and "When a Man Murders . . ." may unintentionally mystify the reader raised in the era of telephonic electronics, digit dialing, and workshops in model mugging. Back in the old days, young reader, answering machines had not yet been invented, telephone exchanges bore evocative names like Rhinelander and Gramercy, and the women who operated switchboards were quaintly known as "girls." In those days, too, a lady who picked up a cigarette thereby compelled the nearest gentleman to offer her a light rather than a lecture on the hazards of second-hand smoke or a query about nicotine patches. I must also inform the young reader that although most of the "females" and "girls" in the world of Nero Wolfe are manipulative, neurotic, mendacious, or vacuous, Rex Stout was not actually scheming to do them in by encouraging them to smoke. As for the method of dealing with "hysterical" women that Archie employs in "When a Man Murders . . . ," I can say only that if Archie tried anything like that today, mystery fiction would lose one of its most engaging narrators.

How, then, does Rex Stout continue to enchant readers of both sexes and all political persuasions? In part by treating men and women alike as objects of critical scrutiny. More important, however, Stout simultaneously confers on the reader—any reader, male or female—so flattering a sense of membership in the vivid quasi family of Wolfe's ménage that the honored adoptee eagerly overlooks, forgives, or treasures the characteristics that define and preserve that orderly universe: Wolfe's misogyny, Archie's women-as-objects chauvinism, even Stout's formulaic plots.

These three witness-centered novellas offer three radically different perspectives on the center of that universe. In "The Next Witness," the agoraphobic, gynephobic Wolfe endures the discomfort of leaving home and suffers the intolerable sensation of finding himself seated next to a "perfumed woman." In contrast, "When a Man Murders . . ." presents the Nero Wolfe most characteristic of the series, the at-home Wolfe who retains his distance from the human specimens that appear before him.

Except in one respect, "Die Like a Dog" is also stock Stout. A murder occurs. So what? The mystery might have been written to illustrate the maxim that nobody cares about the corpse and to refute the theory that the puzzle element accounts for the genre's appeal. The exception is the charming Labrador retriever variously called Jet, Bootsy, and—tellingly, I think—Nero, perhaps the most fleshed-out nonseries character Stout ever created and a dog relegated to none of mystery's hackneyed canine roles. Not the not-quite-victim I had expected, neither is this dog a transparently human character in canine guise. In mystery after mystery, the dog is no character at all but is what psychoanalysts might call a "part object," a nose that sniffs or jaws that menace; or an apparently lifeless possession, a sort of fuzzy umbrella meant to suggest the owner's personality. Ever since "Silver Blaze" dogs have been doing nothing in the night; but in subsequent mysteries countless dogs have done nothing in the daytime, either, thereby creating no incidents, curious or otherwise. Rather, they have sat around like pieces of furniture, perhaps periodically wagging their tails as woofy cuckoo clocks. As objects of fear, dogs have at least come to life, but from the hound of the Baskervilles on, these supposedly menacing creatures have rebelliously endeared themselves to the readers they were supposed to frighten. The hound, for example, is certainly one of Doyle's most popular creations, and Baskerville remains a name lovingly bestowed on gigantic dogs.

Jet, however, is a canine witness portrayed with a

dog lover's enthusiasm and a dog fancier's accuracy. An unmistakably real dog, this rain-loving, hat-fetching creature is equally recognizable as a Labrador retriever, probably a Labrador drawn from life, perhaps even one of Stout's own, as Reed Maroc, Rex Stout's grandson, recently suggested to me. In any case, Stout knew the breed, and Nero Wolfe knows his dogs. In discussing the skull of the Labrador retriever, Wolfe almost quotes the official standard: "wide, giving brain room." Is Wolfe correct in asserting that the Labrador's skull is the widest in dogdom? Perhaps not. But hyperbolic breed loyalty is an absolute mark of the true fancier. With regard to Wolfe's claims about the relative antiquity of the basenji and the Afghan hound, the 1954 edition of the American Kennel Club's *Complete Dog Book* indicates that his was an informed, if arguable, opinion. Furthermore, it is Wolfe's ability to interpret the testimony of the canine witness that really solves the mystery.

Better yet, the dog—Jet, Bootsy, Nero—permits a rare glimpse of an emotional Nero Wolfe and of the boy he once was. Beneath the considerable flesh of the misanthropic gourmand beats the youthful heart of a dog lover, and in the agile and gregarious dog Nero beats the nonneurotic and cholesterol-free heart of the young Wolfe himself. *Nero*, the Italian for "black," the man and the dog, descendant of the wolf, Wolfe and not Wolfe, dog lover, dog fancier. It is thus my pleasure to introduce the great black dog himself: Nero Wolfe.

—Susan Conant

Contents

Three Witnesses

The
Next Witness

I

I had had previous contacts with Assistant District Attorney Irving Mandelbaum, but had never seen him perform in a courtroom. That morning, watching him at the chore of trying to persuade a jury to clamp it on Leonard Ashe for the murder of Marie Willis, I thought he was pretty good and might be better when he had warmed up. A little plump and a little short, bald in front and big-eared, he wasn't impressive to look at, but he was businesslike and self-assured without being cocky, and he had a neat trick of pausing for a moment to look at the jury as if he half expected one of them to offer a helpful suggestion. When he pulled it, not too often, his back was turned to the judge and the defense counsel, so they couldn't see his face, but I could, from where I sat in the audience.

It was the third day of the trial, and he had called his fifth witness, a scared-looking little guy with a pushed-in nose who gave his name, Clyde Bagby, took the oath, sat down, and fixed his scared brown eyes on Mandelbaum as if he had abandoned hope.

Mandelbaum's tone was reassuring. "What is your business, Mr. Bagby?"

The witness swallowed. "I'm the president of Bagby Answers Ink."

"By 'Ink' you mean 'Incorporated'?"

"Yes, sir."

"Do you own the business?"

"I own half the stock that's been issued, and my wife owns the other half."

"How long have you been operating that business?"

"Five years now—nearly five and a half."

"And what is the business? Please tell the jury about it."

Bagby's eyes went left for a quick, nervous glance at the jury box but came right back to the prosecutor. "It's a telephone-answering business, that's all. You know what that is."

"Yes, but some members of the jury may not be familiar with the operation. Please describe it."

The witness licked his lips. "Well, you're a person or a firm or an organization and you have a phone, but you're not always there and you want to know about calls that come in your absence. So you go to a telephone-answering service. There are several dozen of them in New York, some of them spread all over town with neighborhood offices, big operations. My own operation, Bagby Answers Ink, it's not so big because I specialize in serving individuals, houses and apartments, instead of firms or organizations. I've got offices in four different exchange districts—Gramercy, Plaza, Trafalgar, and Rhinelander. I can't work it from one central office because—"

"Excuse me, Mr. Bagby, but we won't go into technical problems. Is one of your offices at six-eighteen East Sixty-ninth Street, Manhattan?"

"Yes, sir."

"Describe the operation at that address."

"Well, that's my newest place, opened only a year ago, and my smallest, so it's not in an office building, it's an apartment—on account of the labor law. You can't have women working in an office building after two a.m. unless it's a public service, but I have to give my clients all-night service, so there on Sixty-ninth Street I've got four operators for the three switchboards, and they all live right there in the apartment. That way I can have one at the boards from eight till two at night, and another one from two o'clock on. After nine in the morning three are on, one for each board, for the daytime load."

"Are the switchboards installed in one of the rooms of the apartment?"

"Yes, sir."

"Tell the jury what one of them is like and how it works."

Bagby darted another nervous glance at the jury box and went back to the prosecutor. "It's a good deal like any board in a big office, with rows of holes for the plugs. Of course it's installed by the telephone company, with the special wiring for connections with my clients' phones. Each board has room for sixty clients. For each client there's a little light and a hole and a card strip with the client's name. When someone dials a client's number his light goes on and a buzz synchronizes with the ringing of the client's phone. How many buzzes the girl counts before she plugs in depends on what client it is. Some of them want her to plug in after three buzzes, some want her to wait longer. I've got one client that has her count fifteen buzzes. That's the kind of specialized individualized service I give my clients. The big outfits, the ones with tens of thousands of clients, they won't do that. They've commercialized it. With me every client is a special case and a sacred trust."

"Thank you, Mr. Bagby." Mandelbaum swiveled his head for a swift sympathetic smile at the jury and swiveled it back again. "But I wasn't buzzing for a plug for your business. When a client's light shows on the board, and the girl has heard the prescribed number of buzzes, she plugs in on the line, is that it?"

I thought Mandelbaum's crack was a little out of place for that setting, where a man was on trial for his life, and turned my head right for a glance at Nero Wolfe to see if he agreed, but one glimpse of his profile told me that he was sticking to his role of a morose martyr and so was in no humor to agree with anyone or anything.

That was to be expected. At that hour of the morning, following his hard-and-fast schedule, he would have been up in the plant rooms on the roof of his old brownstone house on West Thirty-fifth Street, bossing Theodore for the glory of his celebrated collection of orchids, even possibly getting his hands dirty. At eleven o'clock, after washing his hands, he would have taken the elevator down to his office on the ground floor, arranged his oversized corpus in his oversized chair behind his desk, rung for Fritz to bring beer, and started bossing Archie Goodwin, me. He would have given me any instructions he thought timely and desirable, for anything from typing a letter to tailing the mayor, which seemed likely to boost his income and add to his reputation as the best private detective east of San Francisco. And he would have been looking forward to lunch by Fritz.

And all that was "would-have-been" because he had been subpoenaed by the State of New York to appear in court and testify at the trial of Leonard Ashe. He hated to leave his house at all, and particularly he hated to leave it for a trip to a witness-box. Being a private detective, he had to concede that a summons to testify was an occupational hazard he must accept if he hoped to collect fees from clients, but this cloud didn't even have that silver lining. Leonard Ashe had come to the office one day about two months ago to hire him, but had been turned down. So neither fee nor glory was in prospect. As for me, I had been subpoenaed too, but only for insurance, since I wouldn't be called unless Mandelbaum decided Wolfe's testimony needed corroboration, which wasn't likely.

It was no pleasure to look at Wolfe's gloomy phiz, so I looked back at the performers. Bagby was answering. "Yes, sir, she plugs in and says, 'Mrs. Smith's residence,' or, 'Mr. Jones's apartment,' or whatever she has been told to say for that client. Then she says Mrs. Smith is out and is there any message, and so on, whatever the situation calls for. Sometimes the client has called and given her a message for some particular caller." Bagby flipped a hand. "Just anything. We give specialized service."

Mandelbaum nodded. "I think that gives us a clear picture of the operation. Now, Mr. Bagby, please look at that gentleman in the dark blue suit sitting next to the officer. He is the defendant in this trial. Do you know him?"

"Yes, sir. That's Mr. Leonard Ashe."

"When and where did you meet him?"

"In July he came to my office on Forty-seventh Street. First he phoned, and then he came."

"Can you give the day in July?"

"The twelfth. A Monday."

"What did he say?"

"He asked how my answering service worked, and I told him, and he said he wanted it for his home telephone at his apartment on East Seventy-third Street. He paid cash for a month in advance. He wanted twenty-four-hour service."

"Did he want any special service?"

"He didn't ask me for any, but two days later he contacted Marie Willis and offered her five hundred dollars if she—"

The witness was interrupted from two directions at once. The defense attorney, a champion named Jimmy Donovan whose batting average on big criminal cases had topped the list of the New York bar for ten years, left his chair with his mouth open to object; and Mandelbaum showed the witness a palm to stop him.

"Just a minute, Mr. Bagby. Just answer my questions. Did you accept Leonard Ashe as a client?"

"Sure, there was no reason not to."

"What was the number of his telephone at his home?"

"Rhinelander two-three-eight-three-eight."

"Did you give his name and that number a place on one of your switchboards?"

"Yes, sir, one of the three boards at the apartment on East Sixty-ninth Street. That's the Rhinelander district."

"What was the name of the employee who attended that board—the one with Leonard Ashe's number on it?"

"Marie Willis."

A shadow of stir and murmur rippled across the packed audience, and Judge Corbett on the bench turned his head to give it a frown and then went back to his knitting.

Bagby was going on. "Of course at night there's

only one girl on the three boards—they rotate on that —but for daytime I keep a girl at her own board at least five days a week, and six if I can. That way she gets to know her clients."

"And Leonard Ashe's number was on Marie Willis's board?"

"Yes, sir."

"After the routine arrangements for serving Leonard Ashe as a client had been completed, did anything happen to bring him or his number to your personal attention?"

"Yes, sir."

"What and when? First, when?"

Bagby took a second to make sure he had it right before swearing to it. "It was Thursday, three days after Ashe had ordered the service. That was July fifteenth. Marie phoned me at my office and said she wanted to see me privately about something important. I asked if it could wait till she was off the board at six o'clock, and she said yes, and a little after six I went up to Sixty-ninth Street and we went into her room at the apartment. She told me Ashe had phoned her the day before and asked her to meet him somewhere to discuss some details about servicing his number. She told him such a discussion should be with me, but he insisted—"

A pleasant but firm baritone cut in. "If Your Honor pleases." Jimmy Donovan was on his feet. "I submit that the witness may not testify to what Marie Willis and Mr. Ashe said to each other when he was not present."

"Certainly not," Mandelbaum agreed shortly. "He is reporting what Marie Willis told *him* had been said."

Judge Corbett nodded. "That should be kept clear. You understand that, Mr. Bagby?"

"Yes, sir." Bagby bit his lip. "I mean Your Honor."

"Then go ahead. What Miss Willis said to you and you to her."

"Well, she said she had agreed to meet Ashe because he was a theatrical producer and she wanted to be an actress. I hadn't known she was stage-struck but I know it now. So she had gone to his office on Forty-fifth Street as soon as she was off the board, and after he talked some and asked some questions he told her—this is what she told me—he told her he wanted her to listen in on calls to his home number during the day-time. All she would have to do, when his light on her board went on and the buzzes started, if the buzzes stopped and the light went off—that would mean someone had answered the phone at his home—she would plug in and listen to the conversation. Then each evening she would phone him and report. That's what she said Ashe had asked her to do. She said he counted out five hundred dollars in bills and offered them to her and told her he'd give her another thousand if she went along."

Bagby stopped for wind. Mandelbaum prodded him. "Did she say anything else?"

"Yes, sir. She said she knew she should have turned him down flat, but she didn't want to make him sore, so she told him she wanted to think it over for a day or two. Then she said she had slept on it and decided what to do. She said of course she knew that what Ashe was after was phone calls to his wife, and aside from anything else she wouldn't spy on his wife, because his wife was Robina Keane, who had given up her career as an actress two years ago to marry Ashe, and Marie worshiped Robina Keane as her ideal. That's what Marie told me. She said she had decided she must do three things. She must tell me about it because Ashe was my client and she was working for me. She must tell Robina Keane about it, to warn her, because Ashe would probably get someone else to do the spying for him. It occurred to me that her real reason for wanting to tell Robina Keane might be that she hoped—"

Mandelbaum stopped him. "What occurred to you isn't material, Mr. Bagby. Did Marie tell you the third thing she had decided she must do?"

"Yes, sir. That she must tell Ashe that she was going to tell his wife. She said she had to because at the start of her talk with him she had promised Ashe she would keep it confidential, so she had to warn him she was withdrawing her promise."

"Did she say when she intended to do those three things?"

The witness nodded. "She had already done one of them, telling me. She said she had phoned Ashe and told him she would be at his office at seven o'clock. That was crowding it a little, because she had the evening shift that day and would have to be back at the boards at eight o'clock. It crowded me too because it gave me no time to talk her out of it. I went downtown with her in a taxi, to Forty-fifth Street, where Ashe's office was, and did my best but couldn't move her."

"What did you say to her?"

"I tried to get her to lay off. If she went through with her program it might not do any harm to my business, but again it might. I tried to persuade her to let me handle it by going to Ashe and telling him she had told me of his offer and I didn't want him for a client, and then drop it and forget it, but she was dead set on warning Robina Keane, and to do that she had to withdraw her promise to Ashe. I hung on until she entered the elevator to go up to Ashe's office, but I couldn't budge her."

"Did you go up with her?"

"No, that wouldn't have helped any. She was going through with it, and what could I do?"

So, I was thinking to myself, that's how it is. It looked pretty tough to me, and I glanced at Wolfe, but his eyes were closed, so I turned my head the other way to see how the gentleman in the dark blue suit seated next to the officer was taking it. Apparently it looked pretty tough to Leonard Ashe too. With deep creases slanting along the jowls of his dark bony face from the corners of his wide full mouth, and his sunken dark eyes, he was certainly a prime subject for the artists who sketch candidates for the hot seat for the tabloids, and for three days they had been making the most of it. He was no treat for the eyes, and I took mine away from him, to the left, where his wife sat in the front row of the audience.

I had never worshiped Robina Keane as my ideal, but I had liked her fine in a couple of shows, and she was giving a good performance for her first and only courtroom appearance—either being steadfastly loyal to her husband or putting on an act, but good in either case. She was dressed quietly and she sat quietly, but she wasn't trying to pretend she wasn't young and beautiful. Exactly how she and her older and unbeautiful husband stood with each other was anybody's guess, and everybody was guessing. One extreme said he was her whole world and he had been absolutely batty to suspect her of any hoop-rolling; the other extreme said she had quit the stage only to have more time for certain promiscuous activities, and Ashe had been a sap not to know it sooner; and anywhere in between. I wasn't ready to vote. Looking at her, she might have been an angel. Looking at him, it must have taken something drastic to get him that miserable, though I granted that being locked up two months on a charge of murder would have some effect.

Mandelbaum was making sure the jury had got it. "Then you didn't go up to Ashe's office with Marie Willis?"

"No, sir."

"Did you go up later, at any time, after she had gone up?"

"No, sir."

"Did you see Ashe at all that evening?"

"No, sir."

"Did you speak to him on the telephone that evening?"

"No, sir."

Looking at Bagby, and I have looked at a lot of specimens under fire, I decided that either he was telling it straight or he was an expert liar, and he didn't sound like an expert. Mandelbaum went on. "What did you do that evening, after you saw Marie Willis enter the elevator to go up to Ashe's office?"

"I went to keep a dinner date with a friend at a restaurant—Hornby's on Fifty-second Street—and after that, around half-past eight, I went up to my Trafalgar office at Eighty-sixth Street and Broadway. I have six boards there, and a new night girl was on, and I stayed there with her a while and then took a taxi home, across the park to my apartment on East Seventieth Street. Not long after I got home a phone call came from the police to tell me Marie Willis had been found murdered in my Rhinelander office, and I went there as fast as I could go, and there was a crowd out in front, and an officer took me upstairs."

He stopped to swallow, and stuck his chin out a

little. "They hadn't moved her. They had taken the plug cord from around her throat, but they hadn't moved her, and there she was, slumped over on the ledge in front of the board. They wanted me to identify her, and I had—"

The witness wasn't interrupted, but I was. There was a tug at my sleeve, and a whisper in my ear— "We're leaving, come on." And Nero Wolfe arose, sidled past two pairs of knees to the aisle, and headed for the rear of the courtroom. For his bulk he could move quicker and smoother than you would expect, and as I followed him to the door and on out to the corridor we got no attention at all. I was assuming that some vital need had stirred him, like phoning Theodore to tell him or ask him something about an orchid, but he went on past the phone booths to the elevator and pushed the down button. With people all around I asked no questions. He got out at the main floor and made for Centre Street. Out on the sidewalk he backed up against the granite of the courthouse and spoke.

"We want a taxi, but first a word with you."

"No, sir," I said firmly. "First a word *from* me. Mandelbaum may finish with that witness any minute, and the cross-examination may not take long, or Donovan might even reserve it, and you were told you would follow Bagby. If you want a taxi, of course you're going home, and that will just—"

"I'm not going home. I can't."

"Right. If you do you'll merely get hauled back here and also a fat fine for contempt of court. Not to mention me. I'm under subpoena too. I'm going back to the courtroom. Where are you going?"

"To six-eighteen East Sixty-ninth Street."

I goggled at him. "I've always been afraid of this. Does it hurt?"

"Yes. I'll explain on the way."

"I'm going back to the courtroom."

"No. I'll need you."

Like everyone else, I love to feel needed, so I wheeled, crossed the sidewalk, flagged a taxi to the curb, and opened the door. Wolfe came and climbed in, and I followed. After he had got himself braced against the hazards of a carrier on wheels and I had given the driver the address, and we were rolling, I said, "Shoot. I've heard you do a lot of explaining, but this will have to be good."

"It's preposterous," he declared.

"It sure is. Let's go back."

"I mean Mr. Mandelbaum's thesis. I will concede that Mr. Ashe might have murdered that girl. I will concede that his state of mind about his wife might have approached mania, and therefore the motive suggested by that witness might have been adequate provocation. But he's not an imbecile. Under the circumstances as given, and I doubt if Mr. Bagby can be discredited, I refuse to believe he was ass enough to go to that place at that time and kill her. You were present when he called on me that day to hire me. Do you believe it?"

I shook my head. "I pass. You're explaining. However, I read the papers too, and also I've chatted with Lon Cohen of the *Gazette* about it. It doesn't have to be that Ashe went there for the purpose of killing her. His story is that a man phoned him—a voice he didn't recognize—and said if Ashe would meet him at the Bagby place on Sixty-ninth Street he thought they could talk Marie out of it, and Ashe went on the hop, and the door to the office was standing open, and he went in and there she was with a plug cord tight around her throat, and he opened a window and yelled for the police. Of course if you like it that Bagby was lying just now when he said it wasn't him that phoned Ashe, and that Bagby is such a good businessman that he would rather kill an employee than lose a customer—"

"Pfui. It isn't what I like, it's what I don't like. Another thing I didn't like was sitting there on that confounded wooden bench with a smelly woman against me. Soon I was going to be called as a witness, and my testimony would have been effective corroboration of Mr. Bagby's testimony, as you know. It was intolerable. I believe that if Mr. Ashe is convicted of murder on the thesis Mr. Mandelbaum is presenting it will be a justicial transgression, and I will not be a party to it. It wasn't easy to get up and go because I can't go home. If I go home they'll come and drag me out, and into that witness-box."

I eyed him. "Let's see if I get you. You can't bear to help convict Ashe of murder because you doubt if he's guilty, so you're scooting. Right?"

The hackie twisted his head around to inform us through the side of his mouth, "Sure he's guilty."

We ignored it. "That's close enough," Wolfe said.

"Not close enough for me. If you expect me to scoot with you and invite a stiff fine for running out on a subpoena, which you will pay, don't try to guff me. Say we doubt if Ashe is guilty, but we think he may get tagged because we know Mandelbaum wouldn't go to trial without a good case. Say also our bank account needs a shot in the arm, which is true. So we decide to see if we can find something that will push Mandelbaum's nose in, thinking that if Ashe is properly grateful a measly little fine will be nothing. The way to proceed would be for you to think up a batch of errands for me, and you go on home and read a book and have a good lunch, but that's out because they'd come and get you. Therefore we must both do errands. If that's how it stands, it's a fine day and I admit that woman was smelly, but I have a good nose and I think it was Tissot's Passion Flower, which is eighty bucks an ounce. What are we going to do at Sixty-ninth Street?"

"I don't know."

"Good. Neither do I."

II

It was a dump, an old five-story walk-up, brick that had been painted yellow about the time I had started working for Nero Wolfe. In the vestibule I pushed the button that was labeled *Bagby Answers, Inc.*, and when the click came I opened the door and led the way across the crummy little hall to the stairs and up one flight. Mr. Bagby wasn't wasting it on rent. At the front end of the hall a door stood open. As we approached it I stepped aside to let Wolfe go first, since I didn't know whether we were disguised as brush peddlers or as plumbers.

As Wolfe went to speak to a girl at a desk I sent my eyes on a quick survey. It was the scene of the murder. In the front wall of the room three windows overlooked the street. Against the opposite wall were ranged the three switchboards, with three females with headphones seated at them. They had turned their heads for a look at the company.

The girl at the desk, which was near the end window, had only an ordinary desk phone, in addition to a typewriter and other accessories. Wolfe was telling her, "My name is Wolfe and I've just come from the courtroom where Leonard Ashe is being tried." He indicated me with a jerk of his head. "This is my assistant, Mr. Goodwin. We're checking on subpoenas that have been served on witnesses, for both the prosecution and the defense. Have you been served?"

With his air and presence and tone, only one woman in a hundred would have called him, and she wasn't it. Her long, narrow face tilted up to him, she shook her head. "No, I haven't."

"Your name, please?"

"Pearl Fleming."

"Then you weren't working here on July fifteenth."

"No, I was at another office. There was no office desk here then. One of the boards took office calls."

"I see." His tone implied that it was damned lucky for her that he saw. "Are Miss Hart and Miss Velardi and Miss Weltz here?"

My brows wanted to lift, but I kept them down, and anyway there was nothing startling about it. True, it had been weeks since those names had appeared in the papers, but Wolfe never missed a word of an account of a murder, and his skull's filing system was even better than Saul Panzer's.

Pearl Fleming pointed to the switchboards. "That's Miss Hart at the end. Miss Velardi is next to her. Next to Miss Velardi is Miss Yerkes. She came after—she replaced Miss Willis. Miss Weltz isn't here; it's her day off. They've had subpoenas, but—"

She stopped and turned her head. The woman at the end board had removed her headphone, left her seat, and was marching over to us. She was about my age, with sharp brown eyes and flat cheeks and a chin she could have used for an icebreaker if she had been a walrus.

"Aren't you Nero Wolfe, the detective?" she demanded.

"Yes," he assented. "You are Alice Hart?"

She skipped it. "What do you want?"

Wolfe backed up a step. He doesn't like anyone so close to him, especially a woman. "I want information, madam. I want you and Bella Velardi and Helen Weltz to answer some questions."

"We have no information."

"Then I won't get any, but I'm going to try."

"Who sent you here?"

"Autokinesis. There's a cardinal flaw in the assumption that Leonard Ashe killed Marie Willis, and I don't like flaws. It has made me curious, and when I'm curious there is only one cure—the whole truth, and I intend to find it. If I am in time to save Mr. Ashe's life, so much the better; but in any case I have started and will not be stopped. If you and the others refuse to oblige me today there will be other days—and other ways."

From her face it was a toss-up. Her chin stiffened, and for a second she was going to tell him to go soak his head; then her eyes left him for me, and she was going to take it. She turned to the girl at the desk. "Take my board, will you, Pearl? I won't be long." To Wolfe, snapping it: "We'll go to my room. This way." She whirled and started.

"One moment, Miss Hart." Wolfe moved. "A point not covered in the newspaper accounts." He stopped at the boards, behind Bella Velardi at the middle one. "Marie Willis's body was found slumped over on the ledge in front of the switchboard. Presumably she was seated at the switchboard when the murderer arrived. But you live here—you and the others?"

"Yes."

"Then if the murderer was Mr. Ashe, how did he know she was alone on the premises?"

"I don't know. Perhaps she told him she was. Is that the flaw?"

"Good heavens, no. It's conceivable that she did, and they talked, and he waited until a light and buzzes had her busy at the board, with her back to him. It's a minor point, but I prefer someone with surer knowledge that she was alone. Since she was small and slight, even you are not excluded"—he wiggled a finger—"or these others. Not that I am now prepared to charge you with murder."

"I hope not," she snorted, turning. She led the way to a door at the end of the room, on through, and down a narrow hall. As I followed, behind Wolfe, I was thinking that the reaction we were getting seemed a little exaggerated. It would have been natural, under the circumstances, for Miss Velardi and Miss Yerkes to turn in their seats for a good look at us, but they hadn't. They had sat, rigid, staring at their boards. As for Alice Hart, either there had been a pinch of relief in her voice when she asked Wolfe if that was the flaw, or I was in the wrong business.

Her room was a surprise. First, it was big, much bigger than the one in front with the switchboards. Second, I am not Bernard Berenson, but I have noticed things here and there, and the framed splash of red and yellow and blue above the mantel was not only a real van Gogh, it was bigger and better than the one Lily Rowan had. I saw Wolfe spotting it as he lowered himself onto a chair actually big enough for him, and I pulled one around to make a group, facing the couch Miss Hart dropped onto.

As she sat she spoke. "What's the flaw?"

He shook his head. "I'm the inquisitor, Miss Hart,

not you." He aimed a thumb at the van Gogh. "Where did you get that picture?"

She looked at it, and back at him. "That's none of your business."

"It certainly isn't. But here is the situation. You have of course been questioned by the police and the District Attorney's office, but they were restrained by their assumption that Leonard Ashe was the culprit. Since I reject that assumption and must find another in its stead, there can be no limit to my impertinence with you and others who may be involved. Take you and that picture. If you refuse to say where you got it, or if your answer doesn't satisfy me, I'll put a man on it, a competent man, and he'll find out. You can't escape being badgered, madam; the question is whether you suffer it here and now, by me, or face a prolonged inquiry among your friends and associates by meddlesome men. If you prefer the latter don't waste time with me; I'll go and tackle one of the others."

She was tossing up again. From her look at him it seemed just as well that he had his bodyguard along. She tried stalling. "What does it matter where I got that picture?"

"Probably it doesn't. Possibly nothing about you matters. But the picture is a treasure, and this is an odd address for it. Do you own it?"

"Yes. I bought it."

"When?"

"About a year ago. From a dealer."

"The contents of this room are yours?"

"Yes. I like things that—well, this is my extravagance, my only one."

"How long have you been with this firm?"

"Five years."

"What is your salary?"

She was on a tight rein. "Eighty dollars a week."

"Not enough for your extravagance. An inheritance? Alimony? Other income?"

"I have never married. I had some savings, and I wanted—I wanted these things. If you save for fifteen years you have a right to something."

"You have indeed. Where were you the evening that Marie Willis was killed?"

"I was out in Jersey, in a car with a friend—Bella Velardi. To get cooled off—it was a hot night. We got back after midnight."

"In your car?"

"No, Helen Weltz had let us take hers. She has a Jaguar."

My brows went up, and I spoke. "A Jaguar," I told Wolfe, "is quite a machine. You couldn't squeeze into one. Counting taxes and extras, four thousand bucks isn't enough."

His eyes darted to me and back to her. "Of course the police have asked if you know of anyone who might have had a motive for killing Marie Willis. Do you?"

"No." Her rein wasn't so tight.

"Were you friendly with her?"

"Yes, friendly enough."

"Has any client ever asked you to listen in on calls to his number?"

"Certainly not!"

"Did you know Miss Willis wanted to be an actress?"

"Yes, we all knew that."

"Mr. Bagby says he didn't."

Her chin had relaxed a little. "He was her employer. I don't suppose he knew. When did you talk with Mr. Bagby?"

"I didn't. I heard him on the witness stand. Did you know of Miss Willis's regard for Robina Keane?"

"Yes, we all knew that too. Marie did imitations of Robina Keane in her parts."

"When did she tell you of her decision to tell Robina Keane that her husband was going to monitor her telephone?"

Miss Hart frowned. "I didn't say she told me."

"Did she?"

"No."

"Did anyone?"

"Yes, Miss Velardi. Marie had told her. You can ask her."

"I shall. Do you know Guy Unger?"

"Yes, I know him. Not very well."

Wolfe was playing a game I had often watched him at, tossing balls at random to see how they bounced. It's a good way to try to find a lead if you haven't got one, but it may take all day, and he didn't have it. If one of the females in the front room took a notion to phone the cops or the DA's office about us we might have visitors any minute. As for Guy Unger, that was another name from the newspaper accounts. He had been Marie Willis's boy friend, or had he? There had been a difference of opinion among the journalists.

Miss Hart's opinion was that Guy Unger and Marie had enjoyed each other's company, but that was as far as it went—I mean her opinion. She knew nothing of any crisis that might have made Unger want to end the friendship with a plug cord. For another five minutes Wolfe went on with the game, tossing different balls from different angles, and then abruptly arose.

"Very well," he said. "For now. I'll try Miss Velardi."

"I'll send her in." Alice Hart was on her feet, eager

to cooperate. "Her room is next door." She moved. "This way."

Obviously she didn't want to leave us with her van Gogh. There was a lock on a bureau drawer that I could probably have manipulated in twenty seconds, and I would have liked to try my hand on it, but Wolfe was following her out, so I went along—to the right, down the hall to another door, standing open. Leaving us there, she strode on flat heels toward the front. Wolfe passed through the open door with me behind.

This room was different—somewhat smaller, with no van Gogh and the kind of furniture you might expect. The bed hadn't been made, and Wolfe stood and scowled at it a moment, lowered himself gingerly onto a chair too small for him with worn upholstery, and told me curtly, "Look around."

I did so. Bella Velardi was a crack-lover. A closet door and a majority of the drawers in a dressing table and two chests were open to cracks of various widths. One of the reasons I am still shy a wife is the risk of getting a crack-lover. I went and pulled the closet door open, and, having no machete to hack my way into the jungle of duds, swung it back to its crack and stepped across to the library. It was a stack of paperbacks on a little table, the one on top being entitled *One Mistake Too Many*, with a picture of a double-breasted floozie shrinking in terror from a muscle-bound baboon. There was also a pile of recent editions of *Racing Form* and *Track Dope*.

"She's a philanthropist," I told Wolfe. "She donates dough to the cause of equine genetics."

"Meaning?"

"She bets on horse races."

"Does she lose much?"

"She loses. How much depends on what she bets.

Probably tidy sums, since she takes two house journals."

He grunted. "Open drawers. Have one open when she enters. I want to see how much impudence these creatures will tolerate."

I obeyed. The six drawers in the bigger chest all held clothes, and I did no pawing. A good job might have uncovered some giveaway under a pile of nylons, but there wasn't time for it. I closed all the drawers to show her what I thought of cracks. Those in the dressing table were also uninteresting. In the second drawer of the smaller chest, among other items, was a collection of photographs, mostly unmounted snaps, and, running through them, with no expectations, I stopped at one for a second look. It was Bella Velardi and another girl, with a man standing between them, in bathing outfits with the ocean for background. I went and handed it to Wolfe.

"The man?" I asked. "I read newspapers too, and look at the pictures, but it was two months ago, and I could be wrong."

He slanted it to get the best light from a window. He nodded. "Guy Unger." He slipped it into a pocket. "Find more of him."

"If any." I went back to the collection. "But you may not get a chance at her. It's been a good four minutes. Either she's getting a full briefing from Miss Hart, or they've phoned for help, and in that case—"

The sound came of high heels clicking on the uncarpeted hall. I closed the second drawer and pulled the third one open, and was inspecting its contents when the clicks got to the door and were in the room. Shutting it in no hurry and turning to Bella Velardi, I was ready to meet a yelp of indignation, but didn't have to. With her snappy black eyes and sassy little face she must have been perfectly capable of indignation, but her nerves were too busy with something else. She decided to pretend she hadn't caught me with a drawer open, and that was screwy. Added to other things, it made it a cinch that these phone answerers had something on their minds.

Bella Velardi said in a scratchy little voice, "Miss Hart says you want to ask me something," and went and sat on the edge of the unmade bed, with her fingers twisted together.

Wolfe regarded her with his eyes half closed. "Do you know what a hypothetical question is, Miss Velardi?"

"Of course I do."

"I have one for you. If I put three expert investigators on the job of finding out approximately how much you have lost betting on horse races in the past year, how long do you think it would take them?"

"Why, I—" She blinked at him with a fine set of long lashes. "I don't know."

"I do. With luck, five hours. Without it, five days. It would be simpler for you to tell me. How much have you lost?"

She blinked again. "How do you know I've lost anything?"

"I don't. But Mr. Goodwin, who is himself an expert investigator, concluded from publications he found on that table that you are a chronic bettor. If so, there's a fair chance that you keep a record of your gains and losses." He turned to me. "Archie, your search was interrupted. Resume. See if you can find it." Back to her. "At his elbow if you like, Miss Velardi. There is no question of pilfering."

I went to the smaller chest. He was certainly crowding his luck. If she took this without calling a cop she might not be a murderess, but she sure had a tender spot she didn't want touched.

Actually she didn't just sit and take it. As I got a drawer handle to pull it open she loosened her tongue. "Look, Mr. Wolfe, I'm perfectly willing to tell you anything you want to know. Perfectly!" She was leaning toward him, her fingers still twisted. "Miss Hart said I mustn't be surprised at anything you asked, but I was, so I guess I was flustered. There's no secret about my liking to bet on the races, but the amounts I bet— that's different. You see, I have friends who—well, they don't want people to know they bet, so they give me money to bet for them. So it's about a hundred dollars a week, sometimes more, maybe up to two hundred."

If she liked to bet on any animals other than horses, one would have got her ten that she was a damn liar. Evidently Wolfe would have split it with me, since he didn't even bother to ask her the names of the friends.

He merely nodded. "What is your salary?"

"It's only sixty-five, so of course I can't bet much myself."

"Of course. About the windows in that front room. In summer weather, when one of you is on duty there at night, are the windows open?"

She was concentrating. "When it's hot, yes. Usually the one in the middle. If it's very hot, maybe all of them."

"With the shades up?"

"Yes."

"It was hot July fifteenth. Were the windows open that night?"

"I don't know. I wasn't here."

"Where were you?"

"I was out in Jersey, in a car with a friend—Alice Hart. To get cooled off. We got back after midnight."

Wonderful, I thought. That settled that. One woman might conceivably lie, but surely not two.

Wolfe was eying her. "If the windows were open and the shades up the evening of July fifteenth, as they almost certainly were, would anyone in her senses have proceeded to kill Marie Willis so exposed to view? What do you think?"

She didn't call him on the pronoun. "Why, no," she conceded. "That would have been—no, I don't think so."

"Then she—or he—must have closed the windows and drawn the shades before proceeding. How could Leonard Ashe, in the circumstances as given, have managed that without alarming Miss Willis?"

"I don't know. He might have—no, I don't know."

"He might have what?"

"Nothing. I don't know."

"How well do you know Guy Unger?"

"I know him fairly well."

She had been briefed all right. She was expecting that one.

"Have you seen much of him in the past two months?"

"No, very little."

Wolfe reached in his pocket and got the snapshot and held it out. "When was this taken?"

She left the bed and was going to take it, but he held on to it. After a look she said, "Oh, that," and sat down again. All of a sudden she exploded, indignation finally breaking through. "You took that from my drawer! What else did you take?" She sprang up, trembling all over. "Get out of here! Get out and stay out!"

Wolfe returned the snap to his pocket, arose, said,

"Come, Archie, there seems to be a limit after all," and started for the door. I followed.

He was at the sill when she darted past me, grabbed his arm, and took it back. "Wait a minute, I didn't mean that. I flare up like that. I just—I don't care about the damn picture."

Wolfe pulled loose and got a yard of space. "When was it taken?"

"About two weeks ago—two weeks ago Sunday."

"Who is the other woman?"

"Helen Weltz."

"Who took it?"

"A man that was with us."

"His name?"

"His name is Ralph Ingalls."

"Was Guy Unger Miss Weltz's companion, or yours?"

"Why, we—we were just together."

"Nonsense. Two men and two women are never just together. How were you paired?"

"Well—Guy and Helen, and Ralph and me."

Wolfe sent a glance at the chair he had vacated and apparently decided it wasn't worth the trouble of walking back to it. "Then since Miss Willis died Mr. Unger's interest has centered on Miss Weltz?"

"I don't know about 'centered.' They seem to like each other, as far as I know."

"How long have you been working here?"

"At this office, since it opened a year ago. Before that I was at the Trafalgar office for two years."

"When did Miss Willis tell you she was going to tell Robina Keane of her husband's proposal?"

She had expected that one too. "That morning. That Thursday, the fifteenth of July."

"Did you approve?"

"No, I didn't. I thought she ought to just tell him no and forget it. I told her she was asking for trouble and she might get it. But she was so daddled on Robina Keane—" Bella shrugged. "Do you want to sit down?"

"No, thank you. Where is Miss Weltz?"

"This is her day off."

"I know. Where can I find her?"

She opened her mouth and closed it. She opened it again. "I'm not sure. Wait a minute," she said, and went clicking down the hall to the front. It was more like two minutes when she came clicking back and reported, "Miss Hart thinks she's at a little place she rented for the summer up in Westchester. Do you want me to phone and find out?"

"Yes, if you would."

Off she went, and we followed. In the front room the other three were at the boards. While Bella Velardi spoke to Miss Hart, and Miss Hart went to the phone at the desk and got a number and talked, Wolfe stood and frowned around, at the windows, the boards, the phone answerers, and me. When Miss Hart told him Helen Weltz was on the wire he went to the desk and took it.

"Miss Weltz? This is Nero Wolfe. As Miss Hart told you, I'm looking into certain matters connected with the murder of Marie Willis, and would like to see you. I have some other appointments but can adjust them. How long will it take you to get to the city? . . . You can't? . . . I'm afraid I can't wait until tomorrow. . . . No, that's out of the question. . . . I see. You'll be there all afternoon? . . . Very well, I'll do that."

He hung up and asked Miss Hart to tell me how to get to the place in Westchester. She obliged, and beyond Katonah it got so complicated that I got out my notebook. Also I jotted down the phone number. Wolfe had marched out with no amenities, so I thanked her politely and caught up with him halfway down the stairs. When we were out on the sidewalk I inquired, "A taxi to Katonah?"

"No." He was cold with rage. "To the garage for the car."

We headed west.

III

As we stood inside the garage, on Thirty-sixth Street near Tenth Avenue, waiting for Pete to bring the car down, Wolfe came out with something I had been expecting.

"We could walk home," he said, "in four minutes."

I gave him a grin. "Yes, sir. I knew it was coming— while you were on the phone. To go to Katonah we would have to drive. To drive we would have to get the car. To get the car we would have to come to the garage. The garage is so close to home that we might as well go and have lunch first. Once in the house, with the door bolted and not answering the phone, we could reconsider the matter of driving to Westchester. So you told her we would go to Katonah."

"No. It occurred to me in the cab."

"I can't prove it didn't. But I have a suggestion." I nodded at the door to the garage office. "There's a phone in there. Call Fritz first. Or shall I?"

"I suppose so," he muttered, and went to the office door and entered, sat at the desk, and dialed. In a moment he was telling Fritz who and where he was, asking some questions, and getting answers he didn't like. After instructing Fritz to tell callers that he hadn't heard from us and had no idea where we were, and telling him not to expect us home until we got there, he hung up, glared at the phone, and then glared at me.

"There have been four phone calls. One from an officer of the court, one from the District Attorney's office, and two from Inspector Cramer."

"Ouch." I made a face. "The court and the DA, sure, but not Cramer. When you're within a mile of a homicide of his he itches from head to foot. You can imagine what kind of suspicions your walking out under a subpoena would give him. Let's go home. It will be interesting to see whether he has one dick posted out in front, or two or three. Of course he'll collar you and you may get no lunch at all, but what the hell."

"Shut up."

"Yes, sir. Here comes the car."

As we emerged from the office the brown sedan rolled to a stop before us and Pete got out and opened the rear door for Wolfe, who refuses to ride in front because when the crash comes the broken glass will carve him up. I climbed in behind the wheel, released the brake and fingered the lever, and fed gas.

At that time of day the West Side Highway wasn't too crowded, and north of Henry Hudson Bridge, and then on the Sawmill River Parkway, there was nothing to it. I could have let my mind roam if it had had anywhere to roam, but where? I was all for earning a little token of gratitude by jerking Leonard Ashe out from under, but how? It was so damn childish. In his own comfortable chair in his office, Wolfe could usually manage to keep his genius under control, but on the hard courtroom bench, with a perfumed woman crowded against him, knowing he couldn't get up and go home, he had dropped the reins, and now he was stuck. He couldn't call it off and go back to court and apologize because he was too darned pigheaded. He couldn't go home. There was even a chance he couldn't go to Katonah for a wild goose. When I saw in the rear-view mirror a parkway police car closing in on us from behind, I tightened my lips, and when he passed on by and shot ahead I relaxed and took a deep breath. It would have been pretty extreme to broadcast a general alarm for a mere witness AWOL, but the way Cramer felt about Wolfe it wouldn't have been fantastic.

As I slowed down for Hawthorne Circle I told Wolfe it was a quarter to two and I was hungry and what about him, and was instructed to stop somewhere and get cheese and crackers and beer, and a little farther on I obeyed. Parked off a side road, he ate the crackers and drank the beer, but rejected the cheese after one taste. I was too hungry to taste.

The dash clock said 2:38 when, having followed Alice Hart's directions, I turned off a dirt road into a narrow rutted driveway, crawled between thick bushes on both sides, and, reaching an open space, stepped on the brake to keep from rubbing a bright yellow Jaguar. To the left was a gravel walk across some grass that needed mowing, leading to a door in the side of a little white house with blue trim. As I climbed out two people appeared around the corner of the house. The one in front was the right age, the right size, and the right shape, with blue eyes and hair that matched the Jaguar, held back smooth with a yellow ribbon.

She came on. "You're Archie Goodwin? I'm Helen Weltz. Mr. Wolfe? It's a pleasure. This is Guy Unger. Come this way. We'll sit in the shade of the old apple tree."

In my dim memory of his picture in the paper two months back, and in the snap I had found in Bella Velardi's drawer, Guy Unger hadn't looked particularly like a murderer, and in the flesh he didn't fill the bill any better. He looked too mean, with mean little eyes in a big round face. His gray suit had been cut by someone who knew how, to fit his bulgy shoulders, one a little lower than the other. His mouth, if he had opened it wide, would have been just about big enough to poke his thumb in.

The apple tree was from colonial times, with windfalls of its produce scattered around. Wolfe glowered at the chairs with wooden slats which had been painted white the year before, but it was either that or squat, so he engineered himself into one. Helen Weltz asked what we would like to drink, naming four choices, and Wolfe said no, thank you, with cold courtesy. It didn't seem to faze her. She took a chair facing him, gave him a bright, friendly smile, and included me with a glance from her lively blue eyes.

"You didn't give me a chance on the phone," she said, not complaining. "I didn't want you to have a trip for nothing. I can't tell you anything about that awful business, what happened to Marie. I really can't, because I don't know anything. I was out on the Sound on a boat. Didn't she tell you?"

Wolfe grunted. "That's not the kind of thing I'm after, Miss Weltz. Such routine matters as checking alibis have certainly been handled competently by the police, to the limit of their interest. My own interest has been engaged late—I hope not too late—and my attack must be eccentric. For instance, when did Mr. Unger get here?"

"Why, he just—"

"Now, wait a minute." Unger had picked up an unfinished highball from a table next to him and was holding it with the fingertips of both hands. His voice wasn't squeaky, as you would expect, but a thick baritone. "Just forget me. I'm looking on, that's all. I can't say I'm an impartial observer, because I'm partial to Miss Weltz, if that's all right with her."

Wolfe didn't even glance at him. "I'll explain, Miss Weltz, why I ask when Mr. Unger got here. I'll explain fully. When I went to that place on Sixty-ninth Street and spoke with Miss Hart and Miss Velardi I was insufferable, both in manner and in matter, and they should have flouted me and ordered me out, but they didn't. Manifestly they were afraid to, and I intend to learn why. I assume that you know why. I assume that, after I left, Miss Hart phoned you again, described the situation, and discussed with you how best to handle me. I surmise that she also phoned Mr. Unger, or you did, and he was enough concerned about me to hurry to get here before I arrived. Naturally I would consider that significant. It would reinforce my suspicion that—"

"Forget it," Unger cut in. "I heard about you being on your way about ten minutes ago, when I got here. Miss Weltz invited me yesterday to come out this afternoon. I took a train to Katonah, and a taxi."

Wolfe looked at him. "I can't challenge that, Mr. Unger, but it doesn't smother my surmise. On the contrary. I'll probably finish sooner with Miss Weltz if you'll withdraw. For twenty minutes, say?"

"I think I'd better stay."

"Then please don't prolong it with interruptions."

"You behave yourself, Guy," Helen scolded him. She smiled at Wolfe. "I'll tell you what I think, I think he just wants to show you how smart he is. When I told him Nero Wolfe was coming you should have heard him! He said maybe you're famous for brains and he isn't, but he'd like to hear you prove it, something like that. I don't pretend to have brains. I was just scared!"

"Scared of what, Miss Weltz?"

"Scared of you! Wouldn't anybody be scared if they knew you were coming to pump them?" She was appealing to him.

"Not enough to send for help." Wolfe wouldn't enter into the spirit of it. "Certainly not if they had the alternative of snubbing me, as you have. Why don't you choose it? Why do you suffer me?"

"Now *that's* a question." She laughed. "I'll show you why." She got up and took a step, and reached to pat him on the shoulder and then on top of the head. "I didn't want to miss a chance to touch the great Nero Wolfe!" She laughed again, moved to the table and poured herself a healthy dose of bourbon, returned to her chair, and swallowed a good half of it. She shook herself and said, "Brrrrr. That's why!"

Unger was frowning at her. It didn't need the brains of a Nero Wolfe, or even a Guy Unger, to see that her nerves were teetering on an edge as sharp as a knife blade.

"But," Wolfe said dryly, "having touched me, you still suffer me. Of course Miss Hart told you that I reject the thesis that Leonard Ashe killed Marie Willis and propose to discredit it. I'm too late to try any of the conventional lines of inquiry, and anyway they have all been fully and competently explored by the police and the District Attorney on one side and Mr. Ashe's lawyer on the other. Since I can't expect to prove Mr. Ashe's innocence, the best I can hope to establish is a reasonable doubt of his guilt. Can you give it to me?"

"Of course not. How could I?"

"One way would be to suggest someone else with

motive and opportunity. Means is no problem, since the plug cord was there at hand. Can you?"

She giggled, and then was shocked, presumably at herself for giggling about murder. "Sorry," she apologized, "but you're funny. The way they had us down there at the District Attorney's office, and the way they kept after us, asking all about Marie and everybody she knew, and of course what they wanted was to find out if there was anybody besides that man Ashe that might have killed her. But now they're trying Ashe for it, and they wouldn't be trying him if they didn't think they could prove it, and here you come and expect to drag it out of me in twenty minutes. Don't you think that's funny for a famous detective like you? I do."

She picked up her glass and drained it, stiffened to control a shudder, and got up and started for the table. Guy Unger reached and beat her to the bottle. "You've had enough, Helen," he told her gruffly. "Take it easy." She stared down at him a moment, dropped the glass on his lap, and went back to her chair.

Wolfe eyed her. "No, Miss Weltz," he said. "No, I didn't expect to drag a disclosure from you in twenty minutes. The most I expected was support for my belief that you people have common knowledge of something that you don't want revealed, and you have given me that. Now I'll go to work, and I confess I'm not too sanguine. It's quite possible that after I've squandered my resources on it, time and thought and money and energy, and enlisted the help of half a dozen able investigators, I'll find that the matter you people are so nervous about has no bearing on the murder of Marie Willis and so is of no use to me, and of no concern. But I can't know that until I know what it is, so I'm going to know. If you think my process of finding out will cause inconvenience to you and the others, or worse, I suggest that you tell me now. It will—"

"I have nothing to tell you!"

"Nonsense. You're at the edge of hysteria."

"I am not!"

"Take it easy, Helen." Guy Unger focused his mean little eyes on Wolfe. "Look, I don't get this. As I understand it, what you're after is an out for Leonard Ashe on the murder. Is that right?"

"Yes."

"And that's all?"

"Yes."

"Would you mind telling me, did Ashe's lawyer hire you?"

"No."

"Who did?"

"Nobody. I developed a distaste for my function as a witness for the prosecution, along with a doubt of Mr. Ashe's guilt."

"Why doubt his guilt?"

Wolfe's shoulders went up a fraction of an inch, and down again. "Divination. Contrariety."

"I see." Unger pursed his midget mouth, which didn't need pursing. "You're shooting at it on spec." He leaned forward. "Understand me, I don't say that's not your privilege. Of course you have no standing at all, since you admit nobody hired you, but if Miss Weltz tells you to go to hell that won't take you off her neck if you've decided to go to town. She'll answer anything you want to ask her that's connected with the murder, and so will I. We've told the police and the District Attorney, why not you? Do you regard me as a suspect?"

"Yes."

"Okay." He leaned back. "I first met Marie Willis

about a year ago, a little more. I took her out a few times, maybe once a month, and then later a little oftener, to dinner and a show. We weren't engaged to be married, nothing like that. The last week in June, just two weeks before her death, she was on vacation, and four of us went for a cruise on my boat, up the Hudson and Lake Champlain. The other two were friends of mine, a man and a woman—do you want their names?"

"No."

"Well, that was what got me in the murder picture, that week's cruise she had taken on my boat so recently. There was nothing to it, we had just gone to have a good time, but when she was murdered the cops naturally thought I was a good prospect. There was absolutely nothing in my relations with Marie that could possibly have made me want to kill her. Any questions?"

"No."

"And if they had dug up a motive they would have been stuck with it, because I certainly didn't kill her the evening of July fifteenth. That was a Thursday, and at five o'clock that afternoon I was taking my boat through the Harlem River and into the sound, and at ten o'clock that night I was asleep on her at an anchorage near New Haven. My friend Ralph Ingalls was with me, and his wife, and Miss Helen Weltz. Of course the police have checked it, but maybe you don't like the way they check alibis. You're welcome to check it yourself if you care to. Any questions?"

"One or two." Wolfe shifted his fanny on the board slats. "What is your occupation?"

"For God's sake. You haven't even read the papers."

"Yes, I have, but that was weeks ago, and as I remember it they were vague. 'Broker,' I believe. Stockbroker?"

"No, I'm a freewheeler. I'll handle almost anything."

"Have you an office?"

"I don't need one."

"Have you handled any transactions for anyone connected with that business, Bagby Answers, Incorporated? Any kind of transaction?"

Unger cocked his head. "Now that's a funny question. Why do you ask that?"

"Because I suspect the answer is yes."

"Why? Just for curiosity."

"Now, Mr. Unger." Wolfe turned a palm up. "Since apparently you had heard of me, you may know that I dislike riding in cars, even when Mr. Goodwin is driving. Do you suppose I would have made this excursion completely at random? If you find the question embarrassing, don't answer it."

"It's not embarrassing." Unger turned to the table, poured an inch of bourbon in his glass, added two inches of water from a pitcher, gave it a couple of swirls, took a sip, and another one, and finally put the glass down and turned back to Wolfe.

"I'll tell you," he said in a new tone. "This whole business is pretty damn silly. I think you've got hold of some crazy idea somewhere, God knows what, and I want to speak with you privately." He arose. "Let's take a little walk."

Wolfe shook his head. "I don't like conversing on my feet. If you want to say something without a witness, Miss Weltz and Mr. Goodwin can leave us. Archie?"

I stood up. Helen Weltz looked up at Unger, and at me, and then slowly lifted herself from her chair.

"Let's go and pick flowers," I suggested. "Mr. Unger will want me in sight and out of hearing."

She moved. We picked our way through the windfalls of the apple tree, and of two more trees, and went on into a meadow where the grass and other stuff was up to our knees. She was in the lead. "Goldenrod I know," I told her back, "but what are the blue ones?"

No answer. In another hundred yards I tried again. "This is far enough unless he uses a megaphone."

She kept going. "Last call!" I told her. "I admit he would be a maniac to jump Mr. Wolfe under the circumstances, but maybe he is one. I learned long ago that with people involved in a murder case nothing is impossible."

She wheeled on me. "He's not involved in a murder case!"

"He will be before Mr. Wolfe gets through with him."

She plumped down in the grass, crossed her legs, buried her face in her hands, and started to shake. I stood and looked down at her, expecting the appropriate sound effect, but it didn't come. She just went on shaking, which wasn't wholesome. After half a minute of it I squatted in front of her, made contact by taking a firm grip on her bare ankle, and spoke with authority.

"That's no way to do it. Open a valve and let it out. Stretch out and kick and scream. If Unger thinks it's me and flies to the rescue that will give me an excuse to plug him."

She mumbled something. Her hands muffled it, but it sounded like "God help me." The shakes turned into shivers and were tapering off. When she spoke again it came through much better. "You're hurting me," she said, and I loosened my grip on her ankle and in a moment took my hand away, when her hands dropped and she lifted her head.

Her face was flushed, but her eyes were dry. "My God," she said, "it would be wonderful if you put your arms around me tight and told me, 'All right, my darling, I'll take care of everything, just leave it to me.' Oh, that would be wonderful!"

"I may try it," I offered, "if you'll brief me on what I'd have to take care of. The arms around you tight are no problem. Then what?"

She skipped over it. "God," she said bitterly, "am I a fool! You saw my car. My Jaguar."

"Yeah, I saw it. Very fine."

"I'm going to burn it. How do you set fire to a car?"

"Pour gasoline on it, all over inside, toss a match in, and jump back fast. Be careful what you tell the insurance company or you'll end up in the can."

She skipped again. "It wasn't only the car, it was other things too. I had to have them. Why didn't I get me a man? I could have had a dozen, but no, not me. I was going to do it all myself. It was going to be *my* Jaguar. And now here I am, and you, a man I never saw before—it would be heaven if you'd just take me over. I'm telling you, you'd be getting a bargain!"

"I might, at that." I was sympathetic but not mealy. "Don't be too sure you're a bad buy. What are the liabilities?"

She twisted her neck to look across the meadow toward the house. Wolfe and Unger were in their chairs under the apple tree, evidently keeping their voices down, since no sound came, and my ears are good.

She turned back to me. "Is it a bluff? Is he just trying to scare something out of us?"

"No, not just. If he scares something out, fine. If

not, he'll get it the hard way. If there's anything to get he'll get it. If you're sitting on a lid you don't want opened, my advice is to move, the sooner the better, or you may get hurt."

"I'm already hurt!"

"Then hurt worse."

"I guess I can be." She reached for one of the blue flowers and pulled it off with no stem. "You asked what these are. They're wild asters, just the color of my eyes." She crushed it with her fingers and dropped it. "I already know what I'm going to do. I decided walking over here with you. What time is it?"

I looked at my wrist. "Quarter past three."

"Let's see, four hours—five. Where can I see Nero Wolfe around nine o'clock in town?"

From long habit I started to say at his office, but remembered it was out of bounds. "His address and number are in the phone book," I told her, "but he may not be there this evening. Phone and ask for Fritz. Tell him you are the Queen of Hearts, and he'll tell you where Mr. Wolfe is. If you don't say you're the Queen of Hearts he won't tell you anything because Mr. Wolfe hates to be disturbed when he's out. But why not save time and trouble? Evidently you've decided to tell him something, and there he is. Come on and tell him now."

She shook her head. "I can't. I don't dare."

"On account of Unger?"

"Yes."

"If he can ask to speak privately with Mr. Wolfe, why can't you?"

"I tell you I don't dare!"

"We'll go and come back as soon as Unger leaves."

"He's not going to leave. He's going to ride to town with me."

"Then record it on tape and use me for tape. You

can trust my memory. I guarantee to repeat it to Mr. Wolfe word for word. Then when you phone this evening he will have had time—"

"Helen! *Helen!*" Unger was calling her.

She started to scramble up, and I got upright and gave her a hand. As we headed across the meadow she spoke, barely above a whisper. "If you tell him I'll deny it. Are you going to tell him?"

"Wolfe, yes. Unger, no."

"If you do I'll deny it."

"Then I won't."

As we approached they left their chairs. Their expressions indicated that they had not signed a mutual nonaggression pact, but there were no scars of battle. Wolfe said, "We're through here, Archie," and was going. Nobody else said anything, which made it rather stiff. Following Wolfe around the house to the open space, I saw that it would take a lot of maneuvering to turn around without scraping the Jaguar, so I had to back out through the bushes to the dirt road, where I swung the rear around to head the way we had come.

When we had gone half a mile I called back to my rearseat passenger, "I have a little item for you!"

"Stop somewhere," he ordered, louder than necessary. "I can't talk like this."

A little farther on there was roadside room under a tree, and I pulled over and parked.

I twisted around in the seat to face him. "We got a nibble," I said, and reported on Helen Weltz. He started frowning, and when I finished he was frowning more.

"Confound it," he growled, "she was in a panic, and it'll wear off."

"It may," I conceded. "And so? I'll go back and do it over if you'll write me a script."

"Pfui. I don't say I could better it. You are a connoisseur of comely young women. Is she a murderess in a funk trying to wriggle out? Or what is she?"

I shook my head. "I pass. She's trying to wriggle all right, but for out of what I would need six guesses. What did Unger want privately? Is he trying to wriggle too?"

"Yes. He offered me money—five thousand dollars, and then ten thousand."

"For what?"

"Not clearly defined. A retaining fee for investigative services. He was crude about it for a man with brains."

"I'll be damned." I grinned at him. "I've often thought you ought to get around more. Only five hours ago you marched out of that courtroom in the interest of justice, and already you've scared up an offer of ten grand. Of course it may have nothing to do with the murder. What did you tell him?"

"That I resented and scorned his attempt to suborn me."

My brows went up. "He was in a panic, and it'll wear off. Why not string him along?"

"It would take time, and I haven't any. I told him I intend to appear in court tomorrow morning."

"Tomorrow?" I stared. "With what, for God's sake?"

"At the least, with a diversion. If Miss Weltz's panic endures, possibly with something better, though I didn't know that when I was talking with Mr. Unger."

I looked it over. "Uh-huh," I said finally. "You've had a hard day, and soon it will be dark and dinnertime, and then bedtime, and deciding to go back to

court tomorrow makes it possible for you to go home.
Okay, I'll get you there by five o'clock."

I turned and reached for the ignition key, but had
barely touched it when his voice stopped me. "We're
not going home. Mr. Cramer will have a man posted
there all night, probably with a warrant, and I'm not
going to risk it. I had thought of a hotel, but that might
be risky too, and now that Miss Weltz may want to see
me it's out of the question. Isn't Saul's apartment con-
veniently located?"

"Yes, but he has only one bed. Lily Rowan has
plenty of room in her penthouse, and we'd be welcome,
especially you. You remember the time she squirted
perfume on you."

"I do," he said coldly. "We'll manage somehow at
Saul's. Besides, we have errands to do and may need
him. We must of course phone him first. Go ahead. To
the city."

He gripped the strap. I started the engine.

IV

For more years than I have fingers Inspector
Cramer of Homicide had been dreaming of locking
Wolfe up, at least overnight, and that day he darned
near made it. He probably would have if I hadn't spent
an extra dime. Having phoned Saul Panzer, and also
Fritz, from a booth in a drugstore in Washington
Heights, I called the *Gazette* office and got Lon Cohen.
When he heard my voice he said, "Well, well. Are you
calling from your cell?"

"No. If I told you where I am you'd be an accom-
plice. Has our absence been noticed?"

"Certainly, the town's in an uproar. A raging mob

has torn the courthouse down. We're running a fairly good picture of Wolfe, but we need a new one of you. Could you drop in at the studio, say in five minutes?"

"Sure, glad to. But I'm calling to settle a bet. Is there a warrant for us?"

"You're damn right there is. Judge Corbett signed it first thing after lunch. Look, Archie, let me send a man—"

I told him much obliged and hung up. If I hadn't spent that dime and learned there was a warrant, we wouldn't have taken any special precaution as we approached Saul's address on East Thirty-eighth Street and would have run smack into Sergeant Purley Stebbins, and the question of where to spend the night would have been taken off our hands.

It was nearly eight o'clock. Wolfe and I had each disposed of three orders of chili con carne at a little dump on 170th Street where a guy named Dixie knows how to make it, and I had made at least a dozen phone calls trying to get hold of Jimmy Donovan, Leonard Ashe's attorney. That might not have been difficult if I could have left word that Nero Wolfe had something urgent for him, and given a number for him to call, but that wouldn't have been practical, since an attorney is a sworn officer of the law, and he knew there was a warrant out for Wolfe, not to mention me. So I hadn't got him, and as we crawled with the traffic through East Thirty-eighth Street the sight of Wolfe's scowl in the rear-view mirror didn't make the scene any gayer.

My program was to let him out at Saul's address between Lexington and Third, find a place to park the car, and join him at Saul's. But just as I swung over and was braking I saw a familiar broad-shouldered figure on the sidewalk, switched from the brake to the gas pedal, and kept going. Luckily a gap had opened, and the light was green at Third Avenue, so I rolled on through, found a place to stop without blocking traffic, and turned in the seat to tell Wolfe, "I came on by because I decided we don't want to see Saul."

"You did." He was grim. "What flummery is this?"

"No flummery. Sergeant Purley Stebbins was just turning in at the entrance. Thank God it's dark or he would have seen us. Now where?"

"At the entrance of Saul's address?"

"Yes."

A short silence. "You're enjoying this," he said bitterly.

"I am like hell. I'm a fugitive from justice, and I was going to spend the evening at the Polo Grounds watching a ball game. Where now?"

"Confound it. You told Saul about Miss Weltz."

"Yes, sir. I told Fritz that if the Queen of Hearts phones she is to call Saul's number, and I told Saul that you'd rather have an hour alone with her than a blue orchid. You know Saul."

Another silence. He broke it. "You have Mr. Donovan's home address."

"Right. East Seventy-seventh Street."

"How long will it take to drive there?"

"Ten minutes."

"Go ahead."

"Yes, sir. Sit back and relax." I fed gas.

It took only nine minutes at that time of evening, and I found space to park right in the block, between Madison and Park. As we walked to the number a cop gave us a second glance, but Wolfe's size and carriage rated that much notice without any special stimulation. It was just my nerves. There were a canopy and a doorman, and rugs in the lobby. I told the doorman casually, "Donovan. We're expected," but he hung on.

"Yes, sir, but I have orders—Your name, please?"

"Judge Wolfe," Wolfe told him.

"One moment, please."

He disappeared through a door. It was more like five moments before he came back, looking questions but not asking them, and directed us to the elevator. Twelve B, he said.

Getting off at the twelfth floor, we didn't have to look for B because a door at the end of the foyer was standing open, and on the sill was Jimmy Donovan himself. In his shirt sleeves, with no necktie, he looked more like a janitor than a champion of the bar, and he sounded more like one when he blurted, "It's you, huh? What kind of a trick is this? *Judge* Wolfe!"

"No trick." Wolfe was courteous but curt. "I merely evaded vulgar curiosity. I had to see you."

"You can't see me. It's highly improper. You're a witness for the prosecution. Also a warrant has been issued for you, and I'll have to report this."

He was absolutely right. The only thing for him to do was shut the door on us and go to his phone and call the DA's office. My one guess why he didn't, which was all I needed, was that he would have given his shirt, and thrown in a necktie, to know what Wolfe was up to. He didn't shut the door.

"I'm not here," Wolfe said, "as a witness for the prosecution. I don't intend to discuss my testimony with you. As you know, your client, Leonard Ashe, came to me one day in July and wanted to hire me, and I refused. I have become aware of certain facts connected with what he told me that day which I think he should know about, and I want to tell him. I suppose it would be improper for me to tell you more than that, but it wouldn't be improper to tell him. He is on trial for first-degree murder."

I had the feeling I could see Donovan's brain working at it behind his eyes. "It's preposterous," he declared. "You know damn well you can't see him."

"I can if you'll arrange it. That's what I'm here for. You're his counsel. Early tomorrow morning will do, before the court sits. You may of course be present if you wish, but I suppose you would prefer not to. Twenty minutes with him will be enough."

Donovan was chewing his lip. "I can't ask you what you want to tell him."

"I understand that. I won't be on the witness stand, where you can cross-examine me, until tomorrow."

"No." The lawyer's eyes narrowed. "No, you won't. I can't arrange for you to see him; it's out of the question. I shouldn't be talking to you. It will be my duty to report this to Judge Corbett in the morning. Good evening, gentlemen."

He backed up and swung the door shut, but didn't bang it, which was gracious of him. We rang for the elevator, were taken down, and went out and back to the car.

"You'll phone Saul," Wolfe said.

"Yes, sir. His saying he'll report to the judge in the morning meant he didn't intend to phone the DA now, but he might change his mind. I'd rather move a few blocks before phoning."

"Very well. Do you know the address of Mrs. Leonard Ashe's apartment?"

"Yes, Seventy-third Street."

"Go in that direction. I have to see her, and you'd better phone and arrange it."

"You mean now."

"Yes."

"That should be a cinch. She's probably sitting

there hoping a couple of strange detectives will drop in. Do I have to be Judge Goodwin?"

"No. We are ourselves."

As I drove downtown on Park, and east on Seventy-fourth to Third Avenue, and down a block, and west on Seventy-third, I considered the approach to Robina Keane. By not specifying it Wolfe had left it to me, so it was my problem. I thought of a couple of fancy strategies, but by the time I got the car maneuvered to the curb in the only vacant spot between Lexington and Madison I had decided that the simplest was the best. After asking Wolfe if he had any suggestions and getting a no, I walked to Lexington and found a booth in a drugstore.

First I called Saul Panzer. There had been no word from the Queen of Hearts, but she had said around nine o'clock and it was only eight-forty. Sergeant Stebbins had been and gone. What he had said was that the police were concerned about the disappearance of Nero Wolfe because he was an important witness in a murder case, and they were afraid something might have happened to him, especially since Archie Goodwin was also gone. What he had not said was that Inspector Cramer suspected that Wolfe had tramped out of the courtroom hell-bent on messing the case up, and he wanted to get his hands on him quick. Had Wolfe communicated with Saul, and did Saul know where he was? There was a warrant out for both Wolfe and Goodwin. Saul had said no, naturally, and Purley had made some cutting remarks and left.

I dialed another number, and when a female voice answered I told it I would like to speak to Mrs. Ashe. It said Mrs. Ashe was resting and couldn't come to the phone. I said I was speaking for Nero Wolfe and it was urgent and vital. It said Mrs. Ashe absolutely would not come to the phone. I asked it if it had ever heard of Nero Wolfe, and it said of course. All right, I said, tell Mrs. Ashe that he must see her immediately and he can be there in five minutes. That's all I can tell you on the phone, I said, except that if she doesn't see him she'll never stop regretting it. The voice told me to hold the wire, and was gone so long I began to wish I had tried a fancy one, but just as I was reaching for the handle of the booth door to let in some air it came back and said Mrs. Ashe would see Mr. Wolfe. I asked it to instruct the lobby guardians to admit us, hung up, went out and back to the car, and told Wolfe, "Okay. You'd better make it good after what I told her. No word from Helen Weltz. Stebbins only asked some foolish questions and got the answers he deserved."

He climbed out, and we walked to the number. This one was smaller and more elegant, too elegant for rugs. The doorman was practically Laurence Olivier, and the elevator man was his older brother. They were chilly but nothing personal. When we were let out at the sixth floor the elevator man stayed at his open door until we had pushed a button and the apartment door had opened and we had been told to enter.

The woman admitting us wasn't practically Phyllis Jay, she was Phyllis Jay. Having paid $4.40 or $5.50 several times to see her from an orchestra seat, I would have appreciated this free close-up of her on a better occasion, but my mind was occupied. So was hers. Of course she was acting, since actresses always are, but the glamour was turned off because the part didn't call for it. She was playing a support for a friend in need, and kept strictly in character as she relieved Wolfe of his hat and cane and then escorted us into a big living room, across it, and through an arch into a smaller room.

Robina Keane was sitting on a couch, patting at her hair. Wolfe stopped three paces off and bowed. She looked up at him, shook her head as if to dislodge a fly, pressed her fingertips to her eyes, and looked at him again. Phyllis Jay said, "I'll be in the study, Robbie," waited precisely the right interval for a request to stay, didn't get it, and turned and went. Mrs. Ashe invited us to sit, and, after moving a chair around for Wolfe, I took one off at the side.

"I'm dead tired," she said. "I'm so empty, completely empty. I don't think I ever—But what is it? Of course it's something about my husband?"

Either the celebrated lilt of her voice was born in, or she had used it so much and so long that it might as well have been. She looked all in, no doubt of that, but the lilt was there.

"I'll make it as brief as I can," Wolfe told her. "Do you know that I have met your husband? That he called on me one day in July?"

"Yes, I know. I know all about it—now."

"It was to testify about our conversation that day that I was summoned to appear at his trial, by the State. In court this morning, waiting to be called, an idea came to me which I thought merited exploration, and if it was to bring any advantage to your husband the exploration could not wait. So I walked out, with Mr. Goodwin, my assistant, and we have spent the day on that idea."

"What idea?" Her hands were fists, on the couch for props.

"Later for that. We have made some progress, and we may make more tonight. Whether we do or not, I have information that will be of considerable value to your husband. It may not exculpate him, but at least it should raise sufficient doubt in the minds of the jury to get him acquitted. The problem is to get the information to the jury. It would take intricate and prolonged investigation to get it in the form of admissible evidence, and I have in mind a short cut. To take it I must have a talk with your husband."

"But he—How can you?"

"I must. I have just called on Mr. Donovan, his attorney, and asked him to arrange it, but I knew he wouldn't; that was merely to anticipate you. I knew that if I came to you, you would insist on consulting him, and I have already demonstrated the futility of that. I am in contempt of the court, and a warrant has been issued for my arrest. Also I am under subpoena as a witness for the prosecution, and it is improper for the defense counsel even to talk with me, let alone arrange an interview for me with his client. You, as the wife of a man on trial for his life, are under no such prescription. You have wide acquaintance and great personal charm. It would not be too difficult, certainly not impossible, for you to get permission to talk with your husband tomorrow morning before the court convenes; and you can take me with you. Twenty minutes would be ample, and even ten would do. Don't mention me in getting the permission; that's important; simply take me with you and we'll see. If it doesn't work there's another possible expedient. Will you do it?"

She was frowning. "I don't see—You just want to talk with him?"

"Yes."

"What do you want to tell him?"

"You'll hear it tomorrow morning when he does. It's complicated and conjectural. To tell you now might compromise my plan to get it to the jury, and I won't risk it."

"But tell me what it's about. Is it about me?"

Wolfe lifed his shoulders to take in a deep breath, and let them sag again. "You say you're dead tired, madam. So am I. I would be interested in you only if I thought you were implicated in the murder of Marie Willis, and I don't. At considerable risk to my reputation, my self-esteem, and possibly even my bodily freedom, I am undertaking a step which should be useful to your husband and am asking your help; but I am not asking you to risk anything. You have nothing to lose, but I have. Of course I have made an assumption that may not be valid: that, whether you are sincerely devoted to your husband or not, you don't want him convicted of murder. I can't guarantee that I have the key that will free him, but I'm not a novice in these matters."

Her jaw was working. "You didn't have to say that." The lilt was gone. "Whether I'm devoted to my husband. My husband's not a fool, but he acted like one. I love him very dearly, and I want—" Her jaw worked. "I love him very much. No, I don't want him convicted of murder. You're right, I have nothing to lose, nothing more to lose. But if I do this I'll have to tell Mr. Donovan."

"No. You must not. Not only would he forbid it, he would prevent it. This is for you alone."

She abandoned the prop of her fists and straightened her back. "I thought I was too tired to live," she said, lilting again, "and I am, but it's going to be a relief to do something." She left the couch and was on her feet. "I'm going to do it. As you say, I have a wide acquaintance, and I'll do it all right. You go on and make some more progress and leave this to me. Where can I reach you?"

Wolfe turned. "Saul's number, Archie."

I wrote it on a leaf of my notebook and went and

handed it to her. Wolfe arose. "I'll be there all night, Mrs. Ashe, up to nine in the morning, but I hope it will be before that."

I doubted if she heard him. Her mind was so glad to have a job that it had left us entirely. She did go with us to the foyer to see us out, but she wasn't there. I was barely across the threshold when she shut the door.

We went back to the car and headed downtown on Park Avenue. It seemed unlikely that Purley Stebbins had taken it into his head to pay Saul a second call, but a couple of blocks away I stopped to phone, and Saul said no, he was alone. It seemed even more unlikely that Stebbins had posted a man out front, but I stopped twenty yards short of the number and took a good long look. There was a curb space a little further down, and I squeezed the car into it and looked some more before opening the door for Wolfe to climb out. We crossed the street and entered the vestibule, and I pushed the button.

When we left the self-service elevator at the fifth floor Saul was there to greet us. I suppose to some people Saul Panzer is just a little guy with a big nose who always seems to need a shave, but to others, including Wolfe and me, he's the best free-for-all operative that ever tailed a subject. Wolfe had never been at his place before, but I had, many times over the years, mostly on Saturday nights with three or four others for some friendly and ferocious poker. Inside, Wolfe stood and looked around. It was a big room, lighted with two floor lamps and two table lamps. One wall had windows, another was solid with books, and the other two had pictures and shelves that were cluttered with everything from chunks of minerals to walrus tusks. In the far corner was a grand piano.

"A good room," Wolfe said. "Satisfactory. I congratulate you." He crossed to a chair, the nearest thing to his idea of a chair he had seen all day, and sat. "What time is it?"

"Twenty minutes to ten."

"Have you heard from that woman?"

"No, sir. Will you have some beer?"

"I will indeed. If you please."

In the next three hours he accounted for seven bottles. He also handled his share of liver pâté, herring, sturgeon, pickled mushrooms, Tunisian melon, and three kinds of cheese. Saul was certainly prancing as a host, though he is not a prancer. Naturally, the first time Wolfe ate under his roof, and possibly the last, he wanted to give him good grub, that was okay, but I thought the three kinds of cheese was piling it on a little. He sure would be sick of cheese by Saturday. He wasn't equipped to be so fancy about sleeping. Since he was the host it was his problem, and his arrangement was Wolfe in the bedroom, me on the couch in the big room, and him on the floor, which seemed reasonable.

However, at a quarter to one in the morning we were still up. Though time hadn't dragged too heavily, what with talking and eating and drinking and three hot games of checkers between Wolfe and Saul, all draws, we were all yawning. We hadn't turned in because we hadn't heard from Helen Weltz, and there was still a dim hope. The other thing was all set. Just after midnight Robina Keane had phoned and told Wolfe she had it fixed. He was to meet her in Room 917 at 100 Centre Street at half-past eight. He asked me if I knew what Room 917 was, and I didn't. After that came he leaned back in his chair and sat with his eyes closed for a while, then straightened up and told Saul he was ready for the third game of checkers.

At a quarter to one he left his chair, yawned and stretched, and announced, "Her panic wore off. I'm going to bed."

"I'm afraid," Saul apologized, "I have no pajamas you could get into, but I've got—"

The phone rang. I was nearest, and turned and got it. "This is Jackson four-three-one-oh-nine."

"I want— This is the Queen of Hearts."

"It sure is. I recognize your voice. This is Archie Goodwin. Where are you?"

"In a booth at Grand Central. I couldn't get rid of him, and then—but that doesn't matter now. Where are you?"

"In an apartment on Thirty-eighth Street with Mr. Wolfe, waiting for you. It's a short walk. I'll meet you at the information booth, upper level, in five minutes. Will you be there?"

"Yes."

"Sure?"

"Of course I will!"

I hung up, turned, and said loftily, "If it wore off it wore on again. Make some coffee, will you, Saul? She'll need either that or bourbon. And maybe she likes cheese."

I departed.

V

At six minutes past ten in the morning Assistant District Attorney Mandelbaum was standing at the end of his table in the courtroom to address Judge Corbett. The room was packed. The jury was in the box. Jimmy Donovan, defense attorney, looking not at all like a janitor, was fingering through some papers his assistant had handed him.

"Your Honor," Mandelbaum said, "I wish to call a witness whom I called yesterday, but he was not available. I learned only a few minutes ago that he is present. You will remember that on my application you issued a warrant for Mr. Nero Wolfe."

"Yes, I do." The judge cleared his throat. "Is he here?"

"He is." Mandelbaum turned and called, "Nero Wolfe!"

Having arrived at one minute to ten, we wouldn't have been able to get in if we hadn't pushed through to the officer at the door and told him who we were and that we were wanted. He had stared at Wolfe and admitted he recognized him, and let us in, and the attendant had managed to make room for us on a bench just as Judge Corbett entered. When Wolfe was called by Mandelbaum and got up to go forward I had enough space.

He walked down the aisle, through the gate, mounted the stand, turned to face the judge, and stood.

"I have some questions for you, Mr. Wolfe," the judge said, "after you are sworn."

The attendant extended the Book and administered the oath, and Wolfe sat. A witness-chair is supposed to take any size, but that one just barely made it.

The judge spoke. "You knew you were to be called yesterday. You were present, but you left and could not be found, and a warrant was issued for you. Are you represented by counsel?"

"No, sir."

"Why did you leave? You are under oath."

"I was impelled to leave by a motive which I thought imperative. I will of course expound it now if you so order, but I respectfully ask your indulgence. I understand that if my reason for leaving is unsatisfactory I will be in contempt of court and will suffer a penalty. But I ask, Your Honor, does it matter whether I am adjudged in contempt now, or later, after I have testified? Because my reason for leaving is inherent in my testimony, and therefore I would rather plead on the charge of contempt afterwards, if the court will permit. I'll still be here."

"Indeed you will. You're under arrest."

"No, I'm not."

"You're not under arrest?"

"No, sir. I came here voluntarily."

"Well, you are now." The judge turned his head. "Officer, this man is under arrest." He turned back. "Very well. You will answer to the contempt charge later. Proceed, Mr. Mandelbaum."

Mandelbaum approached the chair. "Please tell the jury your name, occupation, and address."

Wolfe turned to the jury box. "I am Nero Wolfe, a licensed private detective, with my office in my house at nine-eighteen West Thirty-fifth Street, Manhattan, New York City."

"Have you ever met the defendant in this case?" Mandelbaum pointed. "That gentleman."

"Yes, sir. Mr. Leonard Ashe."

"Where and under what circumstances did you meet him?"

"He called on me at my office, by appointment, at eleven o'clock in the morning of Tuesday, July thirteenth, this year."

"What did he say to you on that occasion?"

"That he wished to engage my professional services. That he had, the preceding day, arranged for an answering service for the telephone at his residence on

Seventy-third Street in New York. That he had learned, upon inquiry, that one of the employees of the answering service would be assigned to his number and would serve it five or six days a week. That he wanted to hire me to learn the identity of that employee, and to propose to her that she eavesdrop on calls made during the daytime to his number, and report on them either to him or to me—I can't say definitely which, because he wasn't clear on that point."

"Did he say why he wanted to make that arrangement?"

"No. He didn't get that far."

Donovan was up. "Objection, Your Honor. Conclusion of the witness as to the intention of the defendant."

"Strike it," Mandelbaum said amiably. "Strike all of his answer except the word 'No.' Your answer is 'No,' Mr. Wolfe?"

"Yes, sir."

"Did the defendant suggest any inducement to be offered to the employee to get her to do the eavesdropping?"

"He didn't name a sum, but he indicated that—"

"Not what he indicated. What he said."

I allowed myself a grin. Wolfe, who always insisted on precision, who loved to ride others, especially me, for loose talk, and who certainly knew the rules of evidence, had been caught twice. I promised myself to find occasion later to comment on it.

He was unruffled. "He said that he would make it worth her while, meaning the employee, but stated no amount."

"What else did he say?"

"That was about all. The entire conversation was

only a few minutes. As soon as I understand clearly what he wanted to hire me to do, I refused to do it."

"Did you tell him why you refused?"

"Yes, sir."

"What did you say?"

"I said that while it is the function of a detective to pry into people's affairs, I excluded from my field anything connected with marital difficulties and therefore declined his job."

"Had he told you that what he wanted was to spy on his wife?"

"No, sir."

"Then why did you mention marital difficulties to him?"

"Because I had concluded that that was the nature of his concern."

"What else did you say to him?"

Wolfe shifted in the chair. "I would like to be sure I understand the question. Do you mean what I said to him that day, or on a later occasion?"

"I mean that day. There was no later occasion, was there?"

"Yes, sir."

"Are you saying that you had another meeting with the defendant, on another day?"

"Yes, sir."

Mandelbaum held a pose. Since his back was to me I couldn't see his look of surprise, but I didn't have to. In his file was Wolfe's signed statement, saying among other things that he had not seen Leonard Ashe before or since July 13. His voice went up a notch. "When and where did this meeting take place?"

"Shortly after nine o'clock this morning, in this building."

"You met and spoke with the defendant in this building today?"

"Yes, sir."

"Under what circumstances?"

"His wife had arranged to see and speak with him, and she allowed me to accompany her."

"How did she arrange it? With whom?"

"I don't know."

"Was Mr. Donovan, the defense counsel, present?"

"No, sir."

"Who was?"

"Mrs. Ashe, Mr. Ashe, myself, and two armed guards, one at the door and one at the end of the room."

"What room was it?"

"I don't know. There was no number on the door. I think I could lead you to it."

Mandelbaum whirled around and looked at Robina Keane, seated on the front bench. Not being a lawyer, I didn't know whether he could get her to the stand or not. Of course a wife couldn't be summoned to testify against her husband, but I didn't know if this would have come under that ban. Anyway, he either skipped it or postponed it. He asked the judge to allow him a moment and went to the table to speak in an undertone to a colleague. I looked around. I had already spotted Guy Unger, in the middle of the audience on the left. Bella Velardi and Alice Hart were on the other side, next to the aisle. Apparently the Sixty-ninth Street office of Bagby Answers, Inc., was being womaned for the day from other offices. Clyde Bagby, the boss, was a couple of rows in front of Unger. Helen Weltz, the Queen of Hearts, whom I had driven from Saul's address to a hotel seven hours ago, was in the back, not far from me.

The colleague got up and left, in a hurry, and Mandelbaum went back to Wolfe.

"Don't you know," he demanded, "that it is a misdemeanor for a witness for the State to talk with the defendant charged with a felony?"

"No, sir, I don't. I understand it would depend on what was said. I didn't discuss my testimony with Mr. Ashe."

"What did you discuss?"

"Certain matters which I though would be of interest to him."

"What matters? Exactly what did you say?"

I took a deep breath, spread and stretched my fingers, and relaxed. The fat son-of-a-gun had put it over. Having asked that question, Mandelbaum couldn't possibly keep it from the jury unless Jimmy Donovan was a sap, and he wasn't.

Wolfe testified. "I said that yesterday, seated in this room awaiting your convenience, I had formed a surmise that certain questions raised by the murder of Marie Willis had not been sufficiently considered and investigated, and that therefore my role as a witness for the prosecution was an uncomfortable one. I said that I had determined to satisfy myself on certain points; that I knew that in leaving the courtroom I would become liable to a penalty for contempt of court, but that the integrity of justice was more important than my personal ease; that I had been confident that Judge Corbett would—"

"If you please, Mr. Wolfe. You are not now pleading to a charge of contempt."

"No, sir. You asked what I said to Mr. Ashe. He asked what surmise I had formed, and I told him—that it was a double surmise. First, that as one with long experience in the investigation of crime and culprits, I had an appreciable doubt of his guilt. Second, that the police had been so taken by the circumstances pointing to Mr. Ashe—his obvious motive and his discovery of the body—that their attention in other directions had possibly been somewhat dulled. For example, an experienced investigator always has a special eye and ear for any person occupying a privileged position. Such persons are doctors, lawyers, trusted servants, intimate friends, and, of course, close relatives. If one in those categories is a rogue he has peculiar opportunities for his scoundrelism. It occurred to me that—"

"You said all this to Mr. Ashe?"

"Yes, sir. It occurred to me that a telephone-answering service was in the same kind of category as those I have mentioned, as I sat in this room yesterday and heard Mr. Bagby describe the operation of the switchboards. An unscrupulous operator might, by listening in on conversations, obtain various kinds of information that could be turned to account—for instance, about the stock market, about business or professional plans, about a multitude of things. The possibilities would be limitless. Certainly one, and perhaps the most promising, would be the discovery of personal secrets. Most people are wary about discussing or disclosing vital secrets on the telephone, but many are not, and in emergencies caution is often forgotten. It struck me that for getting the kind of information, or at least hints of it, that is most useful and profitable for a blackmailer, a telephone-answering service has potentialities equal to those of a doctor or lawyer or trusted servant. Any operator at the switchboard could simply—"

"This is mere idle speculation, Mr. Wolfe. Did you say all that to the defendant?"

"Yes, sir."

"How long were you with him?"

"Nearly half an hour. I can say a great deal in half an hour."

"No doubt. But the time of the court and jury should not be spent on irrelevancies." Mandelbaum treated the jury to one of his understanding glances, and went back to Wolfe. "You didn't discuss your testimony with the defendant?"

"No, sir."

"Did you make any suggestions to him regarding the conduct of his defense?"

"No, sir. I made no suggestions to him of any kind."

"Did you offer to make any kind of investigation for him as a contribution to his defense?"

"No, sir."

"Then why did you seek this interview with him?"

"One moment." Donovan was on his feet. "I submit, Your Honor, that this is the State's witness, and this is not proper direct examination. Surely it is cross-examination, and I object to it."

Judge Corbett nodded. "The objection is sustained. Mr. Mandelbaum, you know the rules of evidence."

"But I am confronted by an unforeseen contingency."

"He is still your witness. Examine him upon the merits."

"Also, Your Honor, he is in contempt."

"Not yet. That is in abeyance. Proceed."

Mandelbaum looked at Wolfe, glanced at the jury, went to the table and stood a moment gazing down at it, lifted his head, said, "No more questions," and sat down.

Jimmy Donovan arose and stepped forward, but addressed the bench instead of the witness-stand. "Your Honor, I wish to state that I knew nothing of the meeting this morning, of the witness with my client, either before or after it took place. I only learned of it here and now. If you think it desirable, I will take the stand to be questioned about it under oath."

Judge Corbett shook his head. "I don't think so, Mr. Donovan. Not unless developments suggest it."

"At any time, of course." Donovan turned. "Mr. Wolfe, why did you seek an interview this morning with Mr. Ashe?"

Wolfe was relaxed but not smug. "Because I had acquired information which cast a reasonable doubt on his guilt, and I wanted to get it before the court and the jury without delay. As a witness for the prosecution, with a warrant out for my arrest, I was in a difficult situation. It occurred to me that if I saw and talked with Mr. Ashe the fact would probably be disclosed in the course of my examination by Mr. Mandelbaum; and if so, he would almost certainly ask me what had been said. Therefore I wanted to tell Mr. Ashe what I had surmised and what I had discovered. If Mr. Mandelbaum allowed me to tell all I had said to Mr. Ashe, that would do it. If he dismissed me before I finished, I thought it likely that on cross-examination the defense attorney would give me an opportunity to go on." He turned a palm up. "So I sought an interview with Mr. Ashe."

The judge was frowning. One of the jurors made a noise, and the others looked at him. The audience stirred, and someone tittered. I was thinking Wolfe had one hell of a nerve, but he hadn't violated any law I had ever heard of, and Donovan had asked him a plain question and got a plain answer. I would have given a ream of foolscap to see Donovan's face.

If his face showed any reaction to the suggestion

given him, his voice didn't. "Did you say more to Mr. Ashe than you have already testified to?"

"Yes, sir."

"Please tell the jury what you said to him."

"I said that I left this room yesterday morning, deliberately risking a penalty for contempt of court, to explore my surmises. I said that, taking my assistant, Mr. Archie Goodwin, with me, I went to the office of Bagby Answers, Incorporated, on Sixty-ninth Street, where Marie Willis was murdered. I said that from a look at the switchboards I concluded that it would be impossible for any one operator—"

Mandelbaum was up. "Objection, Your Honor. Conclusions of the witness are not admissible."

"He is merely relating," Donovan submitted, "what he said to Mr. Ashe. The Assistant District Attorney asked him to."

"The objection is overruled," Judge Corbett said dryly.

Wolfe resumed. "I said I had concluded that it would be impossible for any one operator to eavesdrop frequently on her lines without the others becoming aware of it, and therefore it must be done collusively if at all. I said that I had spoken at some length with two of the operators, Alice Hart and Bella Velardi, who had been working and living there along with Marie Willis, and had received two encouragements for my surmise: one, that they were visibly disturbed at my declared intention of investigating them fully and ruthlessly, and tolerated my rudeness beyond reason; and two, that it was evident that their personal expenditures greatly exceeded their salaries. I said—may I ask, sir, is it necessary for me to go on repeating that phrase, 'I said'?"

"I think not," Donovan told him. "Not if you confine

yourself strictly to what you said to Mr. Ashe this morning."

"I shall do so. The extravagance in personal expenditures was true also of the third operator who had lived and worked there with Marie Willis, Helen Weltz. It was her day off, and Mr. Goodwin and I drove to her place in the country, near Katonah in Westchester County. She was more disturbed even than the other two; she was almost hysterical. With her was a man named Guy Unger, and he too was disturbed. After I had stated my intention to investigate everyone connected with Bagby Answers, Incorporated, he asked to speak with me privately and offered me ten thousand dollars for services which he did not specify. I gathered that he was trying to bribe me to keep my hands off, and I declined the offer."

"You said all that to Mr. Ashe?"

"Yes, sir. Meanwhile Helen Weltz had spoken privately with Mr. Goodwin, and had told him she wanted to speak with me, but must first get rid of Mr. Unger. She said she would phone my office later. Back in the city, I dared not go to my home, since I was subject to arrest and detention, so Mr. Goodwin and I went to the home of a friend, and Helen Weltz came to us there sometime after midnight. My attack had broken her completely, and she was in terror. She confessed that for years the operation had been used precisely as I had surmised. All of the switchboard operators had been parties to it, including Marie Willis. Their dean, Alice Hart, collected information—"

There was an interruption. Alice Hart, on the aisle, with Bella Velardi next to her, got up and headed for the door, and Bella followed her. Eyes went to them from all directions, including Judge Corbett's, but nobody said or did anything, and when they were five steps from the door I sang out to the guard, "That's Alice Hart in front!"

He blocked them off. Judge Corbett called, "Officer, no one is to leave the room!"

The audience stirred and muttered, and some stood up. The judge banged his gavel and demanded order, but he couldn't very well threaten to have the room cleared. Miss Hart and Miss Velardi gave it up and went back to their seats.

When the room was still the judge spoke to Wolfe. "Go ahead."

He did so. "Alice Hart collected information from them and gave them cash from time to time, in addition to their salaries. Guy Unger and Clyde Bagby also gave them cash occasionally. The largest single amount ever received by Helen Weltz was fifteen hundred dollars, given her about a year ago by Guy Unger. In three years she received a total of approximately fifteen thousand dollars, not counting her salary. She didn't know what use was made of the information she passed on to Alice Hart. She wouldn't admit that she had knowledge that any of it had been used for blackmailing, but she did admit that some of it could have been so used."

"Do you know," Judge Corbett asked him, "where Helen Weltz is now?"

"Yes, sir. She is present. I told her that if she came and faced it the District Attorney might show appreciation for her help."

"Have you anything to add that you told Mr. Ashe this morning?"

"I have, Your Honor. Do you wish me to differentiate clearly between what Helen Weltz told me and my own exposition?"

"No. Anything whatever that you said to Mr. Ashe."

"I told him that the fact that he had tried to hire me to learn the identity of the Bagby operator who would service his number, and to bribe her to eavesdrop on his line, was one of the points that had caused me to doubt his guilt; that I had questioned whether a man who was reluctant to undertake such a chore for himself would be likely to strangle the life out of a woman and then open a window and yell for the police. Also I asked him about the man who telephoned him to say that if Ashe would meet him at the Bagby office on Sixty-ninth Street he thought they could talk Miss Willis out of it. I asked if it was possible that the voice was Bagby's, and Ashe said it was quite possible, but if so he had disguised his voice."

"Had you any evidence that Mr. Bagby made that phone call?"

"No, Your Honor. All I had, besides my assumptions from known facts and my own observations, was what Miss Weltz had told me. One thing she had told me was that Marie Willis had become an imminent threat to the whole conspiracy. She had been ordered by both Unger and Bagby to accept Ashe's proposal to eavesdrop on his line, and not to tell Mrs. Ashe, whom Miss Willis idolized; and she had refused and announced that she was going to quit. Of course that made her an intolerable peril to everyone concerned. The success and security of the operation hinged on the fact that no victim ever had any reason to suspect that Bagby Answers, Incorporated, was responsible for his distress. It was Bagby who got the information, but it was Unger who used it, and the tormented under the screw could not know where the tormentor had got the screw. So Miss Willis's rebellion and decision to quit—combined, according to Miss Weltz, with an implied threat to expose the whole business—were a mortal menace to any and all of them, ample provocation for murder to one willing to risk that extreme. I told Mr. Ashe that all this certainly established a reasonable doubt of his guilt, but I also went beyond that and considered briefly the most likely candidate to replace him. Do you wish that too?"

The judge was intent on him. "Yes. Proceed."

"I told Mr. Ashe that I greatly preferred Mr. Bagby. The mutual alibi of Miss Hart and Miss Velardi might be successfully impeached, but they have it, and besides I have seen and talked with them and was not impressed. I exclude Miss Weltz because when she came to me last evening she had been jolted by consternation into utter candor, or I am a witless gull; and that excludes Mr. Unger too, because Miss Weltz claims certain knowledge that he was on his boat in the Sound all of that evening. As for Mr. Bagby, he had most at stake. He admits that he went to his apartment around the time of the murder, and his apartment is on Seventieth Street, not far from where the murder occurred. I leave the timetable to the police; they are extremely efficient with timetables. Regarding the telephone call, Mr. Ashe said it could have been his voice."

Wolfe pursed his lips. "I think that's all—no, I also told Mr. Ashe that this morning I sent a man, Saul Panzer, to keep an eye on Mr. Bagby's office in Forty-seventh Street, to see that no records are removed or destroyed. I believe that covers it adequately, Your Honor. I would now like to plead to the charge of contempt, both on behalf of Mr. Goodwin and of myself. If I may—"

"No." Judge Corbett was curt. "You know quite

well you have made that charge frivolous by the situation you have created. The charge is dismissed. Are you through with the witness, Mr. Donovan?"

"Yes, Your Honor. No more questions."

"Mr. Mandelbaum?"

The Assistant District Attorney got up and approached the bench. "Your Honor will appreciate that I find myself in an extraordinary predicament." He sounded like a man with a major grievance. "I feel that I am entitled to ask for a recess until the afternoon session, to consider the situation and consult with my colleagues. If my request is granted, I also ask that I be given time, before the recess is called, to arrange for five persons in the room to be taken into custody as material witnesses—Alice Hart, Bella Velardi, Helen Weltz, Guy Unger, and Clyde Bagby."

"Very well." The judge raised his eyes and his voice. "The five persons just named will come forward. The rest of you will keep your seats and preserve order."

All of them obeyed but two. Nero Wolfe left the witness chair and stepped down to the floor, and as he did so Robina Keane sprang up from her place on the front bench, ran to him, threw her arms around his neck, and pressed her cheek against his. As I said before, actresses always act, but I admit that was unrehearsed and may have been artless. In any case, I thoroughly approved, since it indicated that the Ashe family would prove to be properly grateful, which after all was the main point.

VI

The thought may have occurred to you, that's all very nice, and no doubt Ashe sent a handsome check, but after all one reason Wolfe walked out was because he hated to sit against a perfumed woman on a wooden bench waiting for his turn to testify, and he had to do it all over again when the State was ready with its case, against the real murderer. It did look for a while as if he might have to face up to that, but a week before the trial opened he was informed that he wouldn't be needed, and he wasn't. They had plenty without him to persuade a jury to bring in a verdict of guilty against Clyde Bagby.

When a
Man Murders . . .

I

"That's just it," she declared, trying to keep her voice steady. "We're not actually married."

My brows went up. Many a time, seated there at my desk in Nero Wolfe's office, I have put the eye on a female visitor to estimate how many sound reasons she might offer why a wedding ring would be a good buy, but usually I don't bother with those who are already hitched, so my survey of this specimen had been purely professional, especially since her husband was along. Now, however, I changed focus. She would unquestionably grade high, after allowing for the crease in her forehead, the redness around her eyes, and the tension of her jaw muscles, tightening her lips. Making such allowances was nothing new for me, since most of the callers at that office are in trouble, seldom trivial.

Wolfe, who had just come down from the plant rooms in the roof and got his impressive bulk settled in his oversized chair behind his desk, glared at her. "But you told Mr. Goodwin—" he began, stopped, and turned to me. "Archie?"

I nodded. "Yes, sir. A man on the phone said his

name was Paul Aubry, and he and his wife wanted to come to see you as soon as possible, and I told him six o'clock. I didn't tell him to bring their marriage certificate."

"We have one," she said, "but it's no good." She twisted her head around and up. "Tell him, Paul."

She was in the red leather chair near the end of Wolfe's desk. It is roomy, with big arms, and Paul Aubry was perched on one of them, with an arm extended along the top of the back. I had offered him one of the yellow chairs, which are perfectly adequate, but apparently he preferred to stick closer to his wife, if any.

"It's one hell of a mess!" he blurted.

He wasn't red-eyed, but there was evidence that he was sharing the trouble. His hand on top of the chairback was tightened into a fist, his fairly well-arranged face was grim, and his broad shoulders seemed to be hunched in readiness to meet an attack. He bent his head to meet her upward look.

"Don't you want to tell him?" he asked.

She shook her head. "No, you." She put out a hand to touch his knee and then jerked it away.

His eyes went to Wolfe. "We were married six months ago—six months and four days—but now we're not married, according to the law. We're not married because my wife, Caroline—" He paused to look down at her, and, his train of thought interrupted, reached to take her hand, but it moved, and he didn't get it.

He stood up, squared his shoulders, faced Wolfe, and spoke faster and louder. "Four years ago she married a man named Sidney Karnow. A year later he enlisted in the Army and was sent to Korea. A few months later she was officially informed that he was dead—killed in action. A year after that I met her and fell in love with her and asked her to marry me, but she wouldn't until two years had passed since Karnow died, and then she did. Three weeks ago Karnow turned up alive—he phoned his lawyer here from San Francisco—and last week he got his Army discharge, and Sunday, day before yesterday, he came to New York."

Aubry hunched his shoulders like Jack Dempsey ready to move in. "I'm not giving her up," he told the world. "I—will—not—give—her—up!"

Wolfe grunted. "It's fifteen million to one, Mr. Aubry."

"What do you mean, fifteen million?"

"The People of the State of New York. They're lined up against you, officially at least, I'm one of them. Why in heaven's name did you come to me? You should have cleared out with her days ago—Turkey, Australia, Burma, anywhere—if she was willing. It may not be too late if you hurry. Bon voyage."

Aubry stood a moment, took a deep breath, turned and went to the yellow chair I had placed, and sat. Becoming aware that his fists were clenched, he opened them, cupped his hands on his knees, and looked at Caroline. He lifted a hand and let it fall back to his knee. "I can't touch you," he said.

"No," she said. "Not while—no."

"Okay, you tell him. He might think I was bulling it. You tell him."

She shook her head. "He can ask me. I'm right here. Go ahead."

He went to Wolfe. "It's like this. Karnow was an only child, and his parents are both dead, and he inherited a pile, nearly two million dollars. He left a will giving half of it to my—to Caroline, and the other half to some relatives, an aunt and a couple of cousins. His lawyer had the will. After notice of his death came it took several months to get the will probated and the estate distributed, on account of special formalities in a case like that. Caroline's share was a little over nine hundred thousand dollars, and she had it when I met her, and was living on the income. All I had was a job selling automobiles, making around a hundred and fifty a week, but it was her I fell in love with, not the million, just for your information. When we got married it was her idea that I ought to buy an agency, but I'm not saying I fought it. I shopped around and we bought a good one at a bargain, and—"

"What kind of agency?"

"Automobile." Aubry's tone implied that that was the only kind of agency worth mentioning. "Brandon and Hiawatha. It took nearly half of Caroline's capital to swing it, but in the past three months we've cleared over twenty thousand after taxes, and the future was looking rosy—when this happened. I was figuring— but to hell with that, that's sunk. This proposition we want to offer Karnow, it's not my idea and it's not Caroline's, it's ours. It just came out of all our talking and talking after we heard Karnow was alive. Last week we went to Karnow's lawyer, Jim Beebe, to get him to propose it to Karnow, but we couldn't persuade him. He said he knew Karnow too well—he was in college with him—and he knew Karnow wouldn't even listen to it. So we decided—"

"What was the proposal?"

"We thought it was a fair offer. We offered to turn it all over to him, the half-million Caroline has left, and the agency, the whole works, if he would consent to a divorce. Also I would continue to run the agency if he wanted to hire me. Also Caroline would ask for no settlement and no alimony."

"It was my idea," she said.

"It was ours," he insisted.

Wolfe was frowning at them. My brows were up again. Evidently he really was in love with her and not the dough, and I'm all for true love up to a point. As for her, my attitude flopped back to the purely professional. Granting that she was set to ditch her lawful husband, if she felt that her Paul was worth a million bucks to her it would have taken too much time and energy to try to talk her out of it. Cocking an eye at his earnest phiz, which was passable, but no pin-up, I would have said that she was overpricing him.

He was going on. "So when Beebe wouldn't do it and we learned that Karnow had come to New York, we decided I would see him myself and put it up to him. We only decided that last night. I had some business appointments this morning, and this afternoon I went to his hotel—he's at the Churchill—and went up to his room. I didn't phone ahead because I've never seen him, and I wanted to see him before I spoke with him. I wanted a look at him."

Aubry stopped to rub a palm across his forehead, pressing hard. When his hand dropped to his thigh it became a fist again. "One trouble," he said, "was that I wasn't absolutely sure what I was going to say. The main proposition, that was all right, but there were two other things in my mind. The agency is incorporated, and half of the stock is in Caroline's name and half in mine. Well, I could tell him that if he didn't take the offer I would hang on to my half and fight for it, but I hadn't decided whether to or not. The other thing, I could tell him that Caroline is pregnant. It wouldn't have been true, and I guess I wouldn't have said it, but it was in my mind. Anyhow it doesn't matter because I didn't see him."

He clamped his jaw and then relaxed it. "This is where I didn't shine, I admit that, but it wasn't just cold feet. I went up to the door of his room, twenty-three-eighteen, without phoning, and I lifted my hand to knock, but I didn't. Because I realized I was trembling, I was trembling all over. I stood there a while to calm down, but I didn't calm. I realized that if I went in there and put it to him and he said nothing doing, there was no telling what might happen. The way I was feeling I was a lot more apt to queer it than help it. So I just ducked it. I'm not proud of it, but I'm telling you, I gave it a miss and came away. Caroline was waiting for me in a bar down the street, and I went and told her, and that wasn't easy either, telling her I had muffed it. Up to then she had thought I could handle about anything that came along. She thought I was good."

"I still do, Paul," she told him.

"Yeah? I can't touch you."

"Not now. Not until—" Her hand fluttered. "Don't keep saying that."

"Okay, we'll skip it." He went back to Wolfe. "So I told her the man-to-man approach was a bum idea, and we sat and chewed at it. We decided that none of our friends was up to it. The lawyer I use for the agency wouldn't be worth a damn. When one of us thought of you—I forget which—it clicked with both of us, and I went to a booth to phone for an appointment. Maybe you can get him down here and you make him the proposition yourself, or if he won't come you can send Archie Goodwin to see him. Caroline has the idea it might be better to send Goodwin because Karnow's thin-skinned and you might irritate him. We'll leave that to you. I wish I could say if you get him to take our offer you can write your own ticket, any amount you want to make it, but in that case we won't be any too flush so I have to mention it. Five thousand dollars, something like that, we could manage that all right. But for God's sake go to it—now, today, tonight!"

Wolfe cleared his throat. "I'm not a lawyer, Mr. Aubry, I'm a detective."

"I know that, but what's the difference? You have a reputation for getting things out of people. We want you to detect a way of getting Karnow to accept our proposition."

Wolfe grunted. "I could challenge your diction, but you're in no mood to debate semantics. And my fees are based on the kind and amount of work done. Your job seems fairly simple. In describing it to me, how candid have you been?"

"Completely. Absolutely."

"Nonsense. Complete candor is beyond the reach of man or woman. If Mr. Karnow accepts your proposal, can I rely on you to adhere to its terms as you have stated them?"

"Yes. You're damn right you can."

Wolfe's head turned. "Mrs. Karnow, are you—"

"She's not Mrs. Karnow!" Aubrey barked. "She's my wife!"

Wolfe's shoulders went up half an inch and dropped back. "Madam, are you sure you understand the proposal and will faithfully adhere to it?"

"Yes," she said firmly.

"You know that you will be relinquishing a dower right, a legal right, in a large property?"

"Yes."

"Then I must ask a few questions about Mr. Karnow—of you, since Mr. Aubry has never met him. You had no child by him?"

"No."

"You were in love when you married, presumably?"

"We thought—I guess we were. Yes, say we were."

"Did it cool off?"

"Not exactly." She hesitated, deciding how to put it. "Sidney was sensitive and high-strung—you see. I still say 'was' because for so long I thought he was dead. I was only nineteen when we were married, and I suppose I didn't know how to take him. He enlisted in the Army because he thought he ought to, because he hadn't been in the World War and he thought he should do his share of peeling potatoes—that was how he put it—but I didn't agree with him. I had found out by then that what I thought wasn't very important, nor what I felt either. If you're going to try to get him to agree to this of course you want to know what he's like, but I don't really know myself, not after all this time. Maybe it would help for you to read the letters I got from him after he enlisted. He only sent me three, one from Camp Givens and two from Korea—he didn't like writing letters. My husb—Paul said I should bring them along to show you."

She opened her bag, fished in it, and produced some sheets of paper clipped together. I went to get them and hand them to Wolfe, and, since I would probably be elected to deliver the proposal, I planted myself at his elbow and read along with him. All three letters are still in the archives in our office, but I'll present only one, the last one, to give you a sample of the tone and style:

Dear Carrie my true and loving mate I hope:

Pardon me, but my weakness is showing. I would like to be where you are this minute and tell you why I didn't like your new dress, and you would go and put on another one, and we would go to Chambord and eat snails and drink Richebourg and then go to the Velvet Yoke and eat lady fingers and drink tomato soup, and then we would go home and take hot baths and go to sleep on fine linen sheets spread over mattresses three feet thick, covered with an electric blanket. After several days of that I would begin to recognize myself and would put my arms around you and we would drown in delight.

Now I suppose I should tell you enough about this place to make you understand why I would rather be somewhere else, but that would be too easy to bother with, and anyway, as you well know, I hate to write, and especially I hate to try to write what I feel. Since the time is getting closer and closer when I'll try to kill somebody and probably succeed, I've been going through my memory for things about death. Herodotus said, "Death is a delightful hiding-place for weary men." Epictetus said, "What is death but a bugbear?" Montaigne said, "The deadest deaths are the best." I'll quote those to the man I'm going to kill and then he won't mind so much.

Speaking of death, if he should get me instead of me getting him, something I did before I left New York will give you quite a shock. I wish I could be around to see how you take it. You claim you have never worried about money, that it's not worth it. Also you've told me that I always talk sardonic but haven't got it in me to act sardonic. This will show you. I'll admit I have to die to get the last laugh, but that will be sardonic too. I wonder do I love you or hate you? They're hard to tell apart. Remember me in thy dreams.

> Your sardonic
> Kavalier Karnow

As I went to my desk to put the letters under a paperweight Caroline was speaking. "I wrote him two long letters every week. I must have sent him over fifty letters, and he never mentioned them the few times he wrote. I want to try to be fair to him, but he always said he was egocentric, and I guess he was."

"Not was," Aubry said grimly. "*Is.* He *is.*" He asked Wolfe, "Doesn't that letter prove he's a nut?"

"He is—uh—picturesque," Wolfe conceded. He turned to Caroline. "What had he done before he left New York that—upon his death—gave you quite a shock?"

She shook her head. "I don't know. Naturally I thought he had changed his will and left me out. After word came that he was dead I showed that letter to the lawyer, Jim Beebe, and told him what I thought, and he said it did sound like it, but there had been no change made in the will as far as he knew, and Sidney must have been stringing me."

"Not too adroitly," Wolfe objected. "It isn't so simple to disinherit a wife. However, since he didn't try— What do you know about the false report of his death?"

"Only a little from an item in the paper," she said, "but Jim Beebe told me some more. He was left for dead in the field in a retreat, but actually he was only stunned, and he was taken prisoner. He was a prisoner for nearly two years, and then he escaped across the Yalu River, and then he was in Manchuria. By that time he could talk their language—he was wonderful with languages—and he made friends in a village and wore their clothes, and it seems—I'm not sure about this, but apparently he was converted to communism."

"Then he's a jackass," Wolfe asserted.

"Oh, no, he's not a jackass." She was positive. "Maybe he was just being picturesque. Anyhow, a few months after the truce was signed and the fighting stopped he finally decided he had had enough of it and went back across the Yalu and made his way to South Korea and reported to an army post, and they sent him home. And now he's here," She stretched her hands out, at arm's length. "Please, Mr. Wolfe? Please?"

Though of course she didn't know it, that was bad tactics. Wolfe's reaction to an emotional appeal from a man is rarely favorable, and from a woman, never. He turned away from the painful sight, to me. "Archie. You're in my hire, and I can dispatch you on errands within the scope of my métier, but this one isn't. Are you willing to tackle it?"

He was being polite. What he really meant was: Five grand will pay a lot of salaries, including yours, and you will please proceed to earn it for me. So, wishing to be polite too, I suggested a compromise. "I'm willing to go get him and bring him here, and you can tackle it."

"No," he said flatly. "Regarding the proposal as quixotic, as I do, I would be a feeble advocate. I abandon it to your decision."

"I deeply appreciate it," I assured him. "Nuts. If I say no I won't hear the last of it for months, so I'll meet you all the way and say yes. I'll take a shot at it."

"Very well. We'll discuss it after dinner, and in the morning you can—"

They drowned him out, both of them cutting in to protest. They couldn't wait until tomorrow, they had to know. They protested to him and then appealed to me. Why put it off? Why not now? I do not react to emotional appeals the way Wolfe does, and I calmed them down by agreeing with them.

"Very well," Wolfe acquiesced, which was noble of him. "But you must have with you the proposal in writing, in duplicate, signed by Mr. Aubry and—uh—you, madam. You must sign it as Caroline Karnow. Archie. At the bottom, on the left, type the word 'accepted' and a colon. Under the circumstances he would be a nincompoop not to sign it, but it would probably be imprudent to tell him so. Your notebook, please?"

I swiveled and got it from the drawer.

II

I rapped with my knuckles, smartly but not aggressively, on the door of Room 2318 on the twenty-third floor of the Hotel Churchill.

The clients had wanted to camp in Wolfe's office to await word from me, but I had insisted they should be as handy as possible in case developments called for their personal appearance, and they were downstairs in the Tulip Bar, not, I hoped, proceeding to get lit. People in serious trouble have a tendency to eat too little or drink too much, or both.

I knocked again, louder and longer.

On the way in the taxi I had collected a little more information about Sidney Karnow, at least as he had been three years back. His attitude toward money had been somewhat superior, but he had shown no inclination to scatter his pile around regardless. So far as Caroline knew, he hadn't scattered it at all. He had been more than decent about meeting her modest requirements, and even anticipating them. That gave me no lead, but other details did. The key words were "egocentric," which was bad, and "proud," which was good. If he really had pride and wasn't just using it as a cover for something that wouldn't stand daylight, fine. No proud man would want to eat his breakfasts with a woman who was eager to cough up nearly a million bucks for the privilege of eating them with another guy. That, I had decided, was the line to take, but I would have to go easy on the wording until I had sized him up.

Evidently the sizing up would be delayed, since my knocking got no response. Not wanting to risk a picturesque refusal to make an appointment, I hadn't phoned ahead. I decided to go down and tell the clients that patience would be required for ten minutes or ten hours, and take on a sandwich and a glass of milk and then come up for another try, but before I turned away my hand went automatically to the knob for a twist and a push, and the door opened. I stood a second, then pushed it a foot farther, stuck my head in, and called, "Mr. Karnow! Karnow!"

No answer. I swung the door open and crossed the sill. Beyond the light I was letting in was darkness, and I would probably have backed out and shut the door and beat it if I hadn't had such a good nose. When it told me there was a faint odor that I should recognize, and a couple of sniffs confirmed it, I found the wall switch and flipped it, and moved on in. A man was there, spread-eagled on the floor near an open door, flat on his back.

I took a step toward him—that was involuntary—then wheeled and went and closed the door to the hall, and returned. At a glance, from the description Caroline had given me, it was Sidney Karnow. He was dressed, but without a jacket or tie. I squatted and slipped a hand inside his shirt and held my breath; nothing doing. I picked a few fibers from the rug and put them over his nostrils; they didn't move. I got the lashes of his right eye between finger and thumb and pulled the lid partly down; it came stiffly and didn't want to go back. I lifted his hand and pressed hard on the fingernail, and then removed the pressure; it stayed white. Actually I was overdoing it, because the temperature of the skin of his chest had been enough.

I stood up and looked down at him. It was unquestionably Karnow. I looked at my wristwatch and saw 7:22. Through the open door beyond him I could see the glitter of bathroom tiles and fittings, and, detouring around his outstretched arm, I went and squatted again for a close-up of two objects on the floor. One was a GI sidearm, a .45. I didn't touch it. The other was a big wad of bathtowels, and I touched it enough to learn, from a scorched hole and powder black, that it had been used to muffle the gun. I had seen no sign on the body of a bullet's entrance or exit, and to find it I would have had to turn him over, and what did it matter? I got erect and shut my eyes to think. It is my habit, long established, when I open doors where I haven't been invited, to avoid touching the knob with my fingertips. Had I followed it this time? I decided yes. Also, had I flipped the light switch with my knuckle? Again yes. Had I made prints anywhere else? No.

I crossed to the switch and used my knuckle again, got out my handkerchief to open the door and pull it shut after me, took an elevator down to the lobby floor, found a phone booth and dialed a number. The voice that answered belonged to Fritz. I told him I wanted Wolfe.

He was shocked. "But Archie, he's at dinner!"

"Yeah, I know. Tell him I've been trapped by cannibals and they're slicing me, and step on it."

It was a full two minutes before Wolfe's outraged voice came. "Well, Archie?"

"No, sir. Not well. I'm calling from a booth in the Churchill lobby. I left the clients in the bar, went up to Karnow's room, found the door unlocked, and entered. Karnow was on the floor, dead, shot with an army gun. The gun's there, but it wasn't suicide, the gun was muffled with a wad of towels. How do I earn that five grand now?"

"Confound it, in the middle of a meal."

If you think that was put on, you're wrong. I know that damn fat genius. That was how he felt, and he said it, that's all.

I ignored it. "I left nothing in the room," I told him, "and I had no audience, so we're fancy free. I know it's hard to talk with your mouth full, but—"

"Shut up." Silence for four seconds, then: "Did he die within the past ninety minutes?"

"No. The skin on his chest has started to cool off."

"Did you see anything suggestive?"

"No. I was in there maybe three minutes. I wanted to interrupt your dinner. I can go back and give it a whirl."

"Don't." He was curt. "There's nothing to be gained by deferring the discovery. I'll have Fritz notify the police anonymously. Bring Mr. Aubry and Mrs. Karnow—have they eaten?"

"They may be eating now. I told them to."

"See that they eat, and then bring them here on a pretext. Devise one."

"Don't tell them?"

"No. I'll tell them. Have them here in an hour and

ten minutes, not sooner. I've barely started my dinner
—and now this."

He hung up.

After crossing the lobby and proceeding along one
of the long, wide, and luxurious corridors, near the entrance to the Tulip Bar I was stopped by an old acquaintance, Tim Evarts, the first assistant house dick,
only they don't call him that, of the Churchill. He
wanted to chin, but I eased him off. If he had known
that I had just found a corpse in one of his rooms and
forgot to mention it, he wouldn't have been so
chummy.

The big room was only half filled with customers at
that hour. The clients were at a table over in a corner,
and as I approached and Aubry got up to move a chair
for me I gave them both a mark for good conduct. Presumably they were on the sharpest edge of anxiety to
hear what I was bringing, but they didn't yap or claw
at me.

When I was seated I spoke to their waiting faces.
"No answer to my knock. I'll have to try again. Meanwhile let's eat."

I couldn't see that their disappointment was anything but plain, wholesome disappointment.

"I can't eat now," Caroline said wearily.

"I strongly advise it," I told her. "I don't mean a
major meal, but something like a piece of melon and a
sturgeon sandwich? We can get that here. Then I'll try
again, and if there's still no answer we'll see. You can't
stick around here all night."

"He might show up any minute," Aubry suggested.
"Or he might come in and leave again. Wouldn't it be
better if you stayed up there?"

"Not on an empty stomach." I was firm. "And I'll
bet Mrs.— What do I call you?"

"Oh, call me Caroline."

"I'll bet you haven't eaten for a week. You may need some energy, so you'd better refuel."

That was a tough half-hour. She did eat a little, and Aubry cleaned up a turkey sandwich and a hunk of cheese, but she was having a hard time to keep from showing that she thought I was a cold-blooded pig, and Aubry, as the minutes went by, left no doubt of his attitude. It was pretty gloomy. When my coffee cup was empty I told them to sit tight, got up and went out and down the corridor to the men's room, locked myself in a cubicle against the chance that Aubry might appear, and stayed there a quarter of an hour. Then I returned to the bar and went to their table and told them, "No answer. I phoned Mr. Wolfe, and he has an idea and wants to see us right away. Let's go."

"No," Caroline said.

"What for? Aubry demanded.

"Look," I said, "when Mr. Wolfe has an idea and wants me to hear it, I oblige him. So I'm going. You can stay here and soak in the agony, or you can come along. Take your pick."

From their expressions it was a good guess that they were beginning to think that Wolfe was a phony and I was a slob, but since their only alternative was to call the deal off and start hunting another salesman for their line, they had to string along. After Aubry paid the check we left, and in the corridor I steered them to the left and around to an exit on a side street, to avoid the main lobby, because by that time some city employees had certainly responded to Fritz's anonymous phone call to headquarters, and from remarks they had made I had learned that the Aubrys were known at the Churchill. The doorman who waved up a taxi for us called them by name.

At the house I let us in with my key, and, closing the door, shot the chain bolt. As I escorted them down the hall to the office a glance at my wrist told me it was 8:35, so I hadn't quite stretched it to the hour and ten minutes Wolfe had specified, but pretty close. He emerged from the door to the dining room, which is across the hall from the office, stood there while we filed in, and then followed, the look on his face as black as the coffee he had just been sipping. After crossing to his desk and lowering his overwhelming bulk into his chair, he growled at them, "Sit down, please."

They stayed on their feet. Aubry demanded, "What's the big idea? Goodwin says you have one."

"You will please sit down," Wolfe said coldly. "I look at people I'm talking to, especially when I suspect them of trying to flummox me, and my neck is not elastic."

His tone made it evident that what was biting him was nothing trivial. Caroline sidled to the red leather chair and sat on its edge. Aubry plopped on the yellow one and met Wolfe's level gaze.

"You suspect?" he asked quietly. "Who? Of What?"

"I think one of you has seen and talked with Mr. Karnow—today. Perhaps both of you."

"What makes you think so?"

"I reserve that. Whether and when I disclose it depends on you. While complete candor is too much to expect, it should at least be approximated when you're briefing a man for a job you want done. When and where did you see Mr. Karnow, and what was said?"

"I didn't. I have never seen him. I told you that. What's the idea of this?"

Wolfe's head moved. "Then it was you, madam?"

Caroline was staring at him, her brow creased.

"Are you suggesting that I saw my—that I saw Sidney Karnow today?"

"Precisely."

"Well, I didn't! I haven't seen him at all! And I want to know why you're suggesting that!"

"You will." Wolfe rested his elbows on the chair arms, leaned forward, and gave her his straightest and hardest look. She met it. He turned his head to the right and aimed the look at Aubry, and had it met again.

The doorbell rang.

Fritz was in the kitchen doing the dishes, so I got up and went to the hall and flipped the switch of the light out on the stoop and took a look through the one-way glass panel of the front door. What I saw deserved admiration. Sergeant Purley Stebbins of Manhattan Homicide West knew that that panel was one-way glass and he was visible, but he wasn't striking a pose; he just stood there, his big broad pan a foot away from the glass, to him opaque, a dick doing his duty.

I went and opened the door and spoke through the two-inch crack which was all the chain bolt would allow. "Hello there. It wasn't me, honest."

"Okay, comic." His deep bass was a little hoarse, as usual. "Then I won't take you. Let me in."

"For what?"

"I'll tell you. Do you expect me to talk through this damn crack?"

"Yes. If I let you in you'll tramp right over me to bust in on Mr. Wolfe, and he's in a bad humor. So am I. I can spare you ten seconds to loosen up. One, two, three, four—"

He cut me off. "You were just up at the Hotel Churchill. You left there about a half an hour ago with a man named Paul Aubry and his wife, and got into a taxi with them. Where are they? Did you bring them here?"

"May I call you Purley?" I asked.

"You goddam clown."

"All right, then, I won't. After all these years you should know better. Eighty-seven and four-tenths per cent of the people, including licensed detectives, who are asked impertinent questions by cops, answer quick because they are either scared or ignorant of their rights or anxious to cooperate. That lets me out. Give me one reason why I should tell you anything about my movements or any companions I may have had, and make it good."

Silence. After a moment I added, "And don't try to avoid giving me a shock. Since you're Homicide, someone is dead. Who?"

"Who do you think?"

"Huh-uh. I won't try to guess because I might guess the right one and I'd be in the soup."

"I want to be around when you are. Sidney Karnow was killed in his room at the Churchill this afternoon. He had been reported dead in Korea and had just turned up alive, and had learned that his wife had married Paul Aubry. As if I was telling you anything you don't know."

He couldn't see my face through the crack, so I didn't have to bother about managing it. I asked, "Karnow was murdered?"

"That's the idea. He was shot in the back of the head."

"Are you saying I knew about it?"

"Not so far. But you knew about the situation, since you were there with Aubry and the woman. I want 'em, and I want 'em now, and are they here? If not, where are they?"

"I see," I said judiciously. "I admit you have given me a reason. Be seated while I go take a look." I pushed the door shut, went back to the office and crossed to my desk, took a pencil and my memo pad, and wrote:

Stebbins. Says K. murdered. We were seen leaving hotel. Asks are they here and if not where.

I got up to hand it to Wolfe, and he took it in with a glance and slipped it into the top drawer of his desk. He looked at Caroline and then at Aubry. "You don't need me," he told them. "Your problem has been solved for you. Mr. Karnow is dead."

They gawked at him.

"Of course," he added, "you now have another problem, which may be even thornier."

Caroline was stiff, frozen. "I don't believe it," Aubry said harshly.

"It seems authentic," Wolfe declared. "Archie?"

"Yes, sir. Sergeant Stebbins of Homicide is out on the stoop. He says that Karnow was murdered, shot in the back of the head, this afternoon in his room at the Churchill. Mr. Aubry and Mrs. Karnow were seen leaving the hotel with me, and he wants to know if they're here, and if not, where? He says he wants them."

"Good God," Aubry said. Caroline had let out a gasp, but no word. She was still rigid.

Her lips moved, and I thought she asked, "He's dead?" but it was too low to be sure.

Wolfe spoke. "So you have another problem. The police will give you a night of it, and possibly a week or a month. Mr. Stebbins cannot enter this house without a search warrant, and if you were my clients I wouldn't mind letting him wait on the stoop while we considered the matter, but since the job you gave me is now not feasible I am no longer in your hire. I have on occasion welcomed an opportunity to plague the police, but never merely for pastime, so I must bid you good evening."

Caroline had left her chair and gone to Aubry with her hands out, and he had taken them and pulled her to him. Evidently the ban was off.

"However," Wolfe continued, "I have a deep repugnance to letting the police take from my house people who have been moved to consult me and who have not been formally charged with a crime. There is a back way out, leading to Thirty-fourth Street, and Mr. Goodwin will take you by it if you feel that you would like a little time to discuss matters."

"No," Aubry said. "We have nothing to run from. Tell him we're here. Let him in."

Wolfe shook his head. "Not in my house, to drag you out. You're sure you don't want to delay it?"

"Yes."

"Then Archie, will you please handle it?"

I arose, told them, "This way, please," and headed for the door, but stopped and turned when I heard Caroline find her voice behind me.

"Wait a minute," she said, barely loud enough for me to get it. She was standing facing Aubry, gripping his lapels. "Paul, don't you think—shouldn't we ask Mr. Wolfe—"

"There's nothing to ask him." Aubry was up, with an arm across her shoulders. "I've had enough of Wolfe. Come on, Caro mia. We don't have to ask anybody anything."

They came and followed me into the hall. As Aubry

was getting his hat from the rack I opened the door, leaving the chain bolt on, and spoke to Purley. "What do you know, they were right here in the office. That's a break for you. Now if—"

"Open the door!"

"In a moment. Mr. Wolfe is peevish and might irritate you, so if you'll remove yourself, on down to the sidewalk, I'll let them out, and they are yours."

"I'm coming in."

"No. Don't even think of it."

"I want you too."

"Yeah, I thought so. I'll be along shortly. Twentieth Street?"

"Now. With me."

"Again no. I have to ask Mr. Wolfe if there's anything we wouldn't want to bother you with, and if so what. Where do I go, Twentieth Street?"

"Yes, and not tomorrow."

"Right. Glad to oblige. The subjects are here at my elbow, so if you'll just descend the steps—and be careful, don't fall."

He muttered something I didn't catch, turned, and started down. When he was at the bottom of the seven steps I removed the bolt, swung the door open, and told our former clients, "Okay. In return for the sandwiches and coffee, here's a suggestion. Don't answer a single damn question until you have got a lawyer and talked with him. Even if—"

I stopped because my audience was going. Aubry had her arm as they crossed the stoop and started down. Not wishing to give Purley the pleasure of having me watch him take them, I shut the door, replaced the bolt, and returned to the office. Wolfe was leaning back with his eyes closed.

"I'm wanted," I told him. "Do I go?"

"Of course," he growled.

"Are we saving anything?"

"No. There's nothing to save."

"The letters from Karnow to his wife are in my desk. Do I take them and turn them over?"

"No. They are her property, and doubtless she will claim them."

"Did I discover the body?"

"Certainly not. To what purpose?"

"None. Don't worry if I'm late."

I went to the hall for my hat and beat it.

III

Since I wasn't itching to oblige Homicide, and it was a pleasant evening for a walk, I decided to hoof it the fifteen blocks to Twentieth Street, and also to do a little chore on the way. If I had done it in the office Wolfe would have pulled his dignity on me and pretended to be outraged, though he knew as well as I did that it's always desirable to get your name in the paper, provided it's not in the obituary column. So I went to a phone booth in a drugstore on Tenth Avenue, dialed the *Gazette* number, asked for Lon Cohen, and got him.

"Scrap the front page," I told him, "and start over. If you don't want it I'll sell it to the *Times*. Did you happen to know that Paul Aubry and his wife, Mrs. Sidney Karnow to you, called on Nero Wolfe this afternoon, and I went somewhere with them, and brought them back to Mr. Wolfe's office, and fifteen minutes ago Sergeant Purley Stebbins came and got them? Or maybe you don't even know that Karnow was murd—"

"Yeah, I know that. What's the rest of it? Molasses you licked off your fingers?"

"Nope. Guaranteed straight as delivered. I just want to get my employer's name in the paper. Mine is spelled, A-R-C-H—"

"I know that too. Who else has got this?"

"From me, nobody. Only you, son."

"What did they want Wolfe to do?"

Of course that was to be expected. Give a newspaperman an inch and he wants a column. I finally convinced him that that was all for now and resumed my way downtown.

At Manhattan Homicide West on Twentieth Street I was hoping to be assigned to Lieutenant Rowcliff so I could try once more to make him mad enough to stutter, but I got a college graduate named Eisenstadt who presented no challenge. All he wanted was facts, and I dished them out, withholding, naturally, that I had entered the room. It took less than an hour, including having my statement typed and signed, and I declined his pressing invitation to stick around until Inspector Cramer got in. I told him another fact, that I was a citizen in good standing, or fair at least, with a known address, and could be found if and when needed.

Back at the office Wolfe was yawning at a book. The yawn was an act. He wanted to make it clear to me that losing a fee of five grand was nothing to get riled about. I had a choice: either proceed to rile him or go up to bed. They were equally attractive, and I flipped a quarter and caught it. He didn't ask me what I was deciding because he thought I wanted him to. It was heads, and I told him my session at Homicide wasn't worth reporting, said good night, and mounted the two flights to my room.

In the morning, at breakfast in the kitchen, with

Fritz supplying me with hot griddle cakes and the paper propped in front of me, I saw that I had given Lon not one inch but two. He had stretched it because it was exclusive. Aside from that, there was a pile of miscellaneous information, such as that Karnow had an Aunt Margaret named Mrs. Raymond Savage, and she had a son Richard, and a daughter Ann, now married to one Norman Horne. There was a picture of Ann, and also one of Caroline, not very good.

I seldom see Wolfe in the morning until eleven, when he comes down from the plant rooms, and that morning I didn't see him at all. A little after ten a call came from Sergeant Stebbins to invite me to drop in at the District Attorney's office at my earliest inconvenience. I don't apologize for taking only four minutes to put weights on papers on my desk, phone up to Wolfe, and get my hat and go, because there was a chance of running into our former clients, and they might possibly be coming to the conclusion that they hadn't had enough of Wolfe after all.

I needn't have been in such a hurry. In a large anteroom on an upper floor at 155 Leonard Street I sat for nearly half an hour on a hard wooden chair, waiting. I was about ready to go over to the window and tell the veteran female that another three minutes was all I could spare when another female appeared, coming from a corridor that led within. That one was not veteran at all, and I postponed my ultimatum. The way she moved was worthy of study, her face invited a full analysis, her clothes deserved a complete inventory, and either her name was Ann Savage Horne or the *Gazette* had run the wrong picture.

She saw me taking her in, and reciprocated frankly, her head tilted a little to one side, came and sat on a chair near mine, and gave me the kind of straight look that you expect only from a queen or a trollop.

I spoke. "What's that stole?" I asked her. "Rabbit?"

She smiled to dazzle me and darned near made it. "Where did you get the idea," she asked back, "that vulgarity is the best policy?"

"It's not policy; I was born vulgar. When I saw your picture in the paper I wondered what your voice was like, and I wanted to hear it. Talk some more."

"Oh. You're one up on me."

"I don't mind squaring it. I am called Goodwin, Archie Goodwin."

"Goodwin?" she frowned a little. She brightened. "Of course! You're in the paper too—if you're that one. You work for Nero Wolfe?"

"I practically *am* Nero Wolfe, when it comes to work. Where were you yesterday afternoon from eleven minutes past two until eighteen minutes to six?"

"Let's see. I was walking in the park with my pet flamingo. If you think that's no alibi, you're wrong. My flamingo can talk. Ask me some more."

"Can your flamingo tell time?"

"Certainly. It wears a wristwatch on its neck."

"How can it see it?"

She nodded. "I knew you'd ask that. It has been trained to tie its neck in a knot, just a plain single knot, and when it does that the watch is on a bend so that— well, Mother?" She was suddenly out of her chair and moving. "What, no handcuffs on anybody?"

Mother, Sidney Karnow's Aunt Margaret, leading a procession emerging from the corridor, would have made two of her daughter Ann and more than half of Nero Wolfe. She was large not only in bulk but also in facial detail, each and all of her features being so big

that space above her chin was at a premium. Besides
her was a thin young man, runty by comparison, wearing black-rimmed glasses, and behind them were two
other males, one, obviously, from his resemblance to
Mother, Ann's brother Richard, and the other a tall
loose-jointed specimen who would have been called
distinguished-looking by any woman between sixteen
and sixty.

As I made my swift survey the flamingo trainer
was going on. "Mother, this is Mr. Goodwin—the Archie Goodwin who was at the Churchill yesterday with
Caroline and Paul. He's grilling me. Mr. Goodwin, my
mother, my brother Dick, my husband, Norman Horne
—no, not the one with the cheaters, that's Jim Beebe,
the lawyer to end all laws. *This* is my husband." The
distinguished-looking one had pushed by and was
beside her. She was flowing on. "You know how disappointed I was at the District Attorney being so god-
awful polite to us, but Mr. Goodwin is different. He's
going to give me the third degree—physically, I mean;
he's built for it, and I expect I'll go to pieces and confess—"

Her husband's palm pressed over her mouth, firm
but not rough, stopped her. "You talk too much, darling," he said tolerantly.

"It's her sense of humor," Aunt Margaret explained. "All the same, Ann dear, it *is* out of place, with
poor Sidney just cruelly murdered. *Cruelly.*"

"Nuts," Dick Savage snapped.

"It *was* cruel," his mother insisted. "Murder *is*
cruel."

"Sure it was," he agreed, "but for us Sid has been
dead more than two years, and he's been alive again
only two weeks, and we never even saw him, so what
do you expect?"

"I suggest," Beebe the lawyer put in, in a high thin voice that fitted his stature perfectly, "that this is rather a public spot for a private discussion. Shall we go?"

"I can't," Ann declared. "Mr. Goodwin is going to wear me down and finally break me. Look at his hard gray eyes. Look at his jaw."

"Now, darling," Norman Horne said affectionately, and took her elbow and started her toward the door. The others filed after them, with Beebe in the rear. Not one mentioned the pleasure it had given them to meet me, though the lawyer did let me have a nod of farewell as he went by.

As I stood and watched the door closing behind them the veteran female's voice came. "Mr. Mandelbaum will see you, Mr. Goodwin."

Only two assistant district attorneys rate corner rooms, and Mandelbaum wasn't one of them. Halfway down the corridor, his door was standing open, and, entering, I had a surprise. Mandelbaum was at his desk, and across from him, on one of the two spare chairs that the little room sported, was a big husky guy with graying hair, a broad red face, and gray eyes that had been found hard to meet by tougher babies than Mrs. Norman Horne. If she called mine hard she should have seen those of Inspector Cramer of Homicide.

"I'm honored," I said appreciatively and accepted Mandelbaum's invitation to use the third chair.

"Look at me," Cramer commanded.

I did so with my brows up, which always annoys him.

"I'm late for an appointment," he said, "so I'll cut it short. I've just been up to see Wolfe. Of course he corroborates you, and he says he has no client. I've read your statement. I tell you frankly that we have no proof that you entered that hotel room."

"Now I can breathe again," I said with feeling.

"Yeah. The day you stop I'll eat as usual. I admit we have no proof, as yet, that you went in that room, but I know damn well you did. Information that the body was there came to us over the phone in a voice that was obviously disguised. You won't deny that I know pretty well by now how you react to situations."

"Sure. Boldly, bravely, and brilliantly."

"I only say I know. Leaving Aubry and Mrs. Karnow down in the bar, you go up and knock on the door of Karnow's room, and get no answer. In that situation there's not one chance in a thousand that you would leave without trying the knob."

"Then I must have."

"So you did?"

I stayed patient and reasonable. "Either I didn't try the knob—"

"Can it. Of course you did, and you found the door wasn't locked. So you opened it and called Karnow's name and got no answer, and you went in and saw the body. That I know, because I know you, and also because of what followed. You went back down to the bar and sat with them a while, and then took them back to Wolfe. Why? Because you knew Karnow had been murdered. If you had merely gone away when your knock wasn't answered, you would have stuck there until Karnow showed, if it took all night. And that's not half of it. When Stebbins went to Wolfe's place after them, with no warrant and no charge entered, Wolfe meekly handed them over! He says they were no longer his clients, since Stebbins had brought the news that Karnow was dead, but why weren't they? Because he won't take a murderer for a client knowingly, and he thought Aubry had killed Karnow. That's why."

I shook my head. "Gee, if you already know everything, I don't see why you bother with me."

"I want to know exactly what you did in that room, and whether you changed anything or took anything." Cramer leaned to me. "Look, Goodwin, I advise you to unload. The way it's going, I fully expect Aubry to break before the day's out, and when he does we'll have it all, including what you told them you had seen in Karnow's room when you rejoined them in the bar, and why the three of you went back to Wolfe's place. If you let me have it now I won't hold it against you that — What are you grinning for?"

"I'm thinking of Mr. Wolfe's face when I tell him this. When Stebbins came with the news that Karnow was dead, and therefore the job was up the flue, Mr. Wolfe hinted as far as his dignity would let him that he would consider another job if they had one, but they sidestepped it. So this will upset him. He keeps telling me we mustn't get discouraged, that some day you will be right about something, but this will be a blow—"

Cramer got up and tramped from the room.

I let Mandelbaum have the tail end of the grin. "Is he getting more sensitive?"

"Someday," the Assistant DA declared, "certain people are going to decide that Wolfe and you are doing more harm than good, and you won't have so much fun without a license. I'm too busy to play games. Please beat it."

When I got back to Thirty-fifth Street, a little after noon, Wolfe was at his desk, fiddling with stacks of cards from the files, plant germination records. I asked if he wanted a report of my visit with Mandelbaum and Cramer, and he said none was needed because he had talked with Cramer and knew the nature of his current befuddlement. I said I had met Karnow's relatives and also his lawyer, and would he care for my impressions, and got no reply but a rude grunt, so I passed it and went to my desk to finish some chores that had been interrupted by Stebbins' phone call. I had just started in when the doorbell rang, and I went to the hall to answer it.

Caroline Karnow was there on the stoop. I went and opened the door, and she stepped in.

"I want to see Mr. Wolfe," she blurted, and proved it by going right on, to the office door and in. I am supposed to block visitors until I learn if Wolfe will see them, but it would have taken a flying tackle, and I let her go and merely followed. By the time I got there she was in the red leather chair as if she owned it.

Wolfe, a germination card in each hand, was scowling at her.

"They've arrested him," she said. "For murder."

"Naturally," Wolfe growled.

"But he didn't do it!"

"Also naturally. I mean naturally you would say that."

"But it's true! I want you to prove it."

Wolfe shook his head. "Not required. They must prove he did. You're all tight, madam. Too tight. Have you eaten today?"

"Good lord," she said, "all you two think about is eating. Last night him, and now—" She started to laugh, at first a sort of gurgle, and then really out with it. I got up and went to her, took her head between my hands to turn her face up, and kissed her on the lips unmistakably. With some customers that is more satisfactory than a slap, and just as effective. I paid no attention to her first convulsive jerks, and released her head only when she quit shaking and got hold of my hair. I pulled loose and backed up a step.

"What on earth—" She gasped.

I decided she had snapped out of it, went to the kitchen and asked Fritz to bring crackers and milk and hot coffee, and returned. As I sat at my desk she demanded, "Did you have to do that?"

"Look," I said, "evidently you came to get Mr. Wolfe to help you. He can't stand hysterical women, and in another four seconds he would have been out of the room and would have refused to see you again. That's one angle of it. I am going on talking to give both you and Mr. Wolfe a chance to calm down. Another angle is that if you think it's undesirable to be kissed by me I am willing to submit it to a vote by people who ought to know."

She was passing her hands over her hair. "I suppose I should thank you?"

"You're welcome."

"Are you recovered," Wolfe rasped, "or not?"

"I'm all right." She swallowed. "I haven't slept, and it's quite true I haven't eaten anything, but I'm all right. They've arrested Paul for murder. He wants me to get a lawyer, and of course I have to, but I don't know who. The one he uses in business is no good for this, and certainly Jim Beebe won't do, and two other lawyers I know—I don't think they're much good. I told Paul I was coming to you, and he said all right."

"You want me to recommend a lawyer?"

"Yes, but we want you too. We want you to do— well, whatever you do." Suddenly she was flushing, and the color was good for her face. "Paul says you charge very high, but I suppose I have lots of money again, now that Sidney is dead." The flush deepened. "I've got to tell you something. Last night when you told us about it, that Sidney had been murdered, for just one second I thought Paul had done it—one awful second."

"I know you did. Only I would say ten seconds. Then you went to him."

"Yes. I went and touched him and let him touch me, and then it was over, but it was horrible. And that's partly why I must ask you, do you believe Paul killed him?"

"No," Wolfe said flatly.

"You're not just saying that?"

"I never just say anything." Wolfe suddenly realized that he had swiveled his chair away from her when she started to erupt, and now swung it back. "Mr. Cramer, a policeman, came this morning and twitted me for having let a murderer hoodwink me. When he had gone I considered the matter. It would have to be that Mr. Aubry, having killed Mr. Karnow, and having discussed it with you, decided to come and engage me to deal with Karnow in order to establish the fact that he didn't know Karnow was dead. That is Mr. Cramer's position, and I reject it. I sat here for an hour yesterday, listening to Mr. Aubry and looking at him, and if he had just come from killing the man he was asking me to deal with, I am a dolt. Since I am not a dolt, Mr. Aubry is not a murderer. Therefore—Yes, Fritz. Here's something for you, madam."

I would like to think it was my kiss that gave her an appetite, but I suppose it was the assurance from Wolfe that he didn't think her Paul was guilty of murder. She disposed not only of the crackers and milk but also of a healthy portion of toast spread with Fritz's liver pâté and chives, while Wolfe busied himself with the cards and I found something to do on my desk.

"I do thank you," she said. "This is wonderful coffee. I feel better."

It is so agreeable to Wolfe to have someone enjoy food that he had almost forgiven her for losing control. He nearly smiled at her.

"You must understand," he said gruffly, "that if you hire me to investigate there are no reservations. I think Mr. Aubry is innocent, but if I find he isn't I am committed to no evasion or concealment. You understand that?"

"Yes. I don't—All right."

"For counsel I suggest Nathaniel Parker. Inquire about him if you wish; if you settle on him we'll arrange an appointment. Now, if Mr. Aubry didn't kill Karnow, who did?"

No reply.

"Well?" Wolfe demanded.

She put the coffee cup down. "Are you asking me?"

"Yes."

"I don't know."

"Then we'll return to that. You said Mr. Aubry has been arrested for murder. Has that charge been entered, or is he being held as a material witness?"

"No, murder. They said I couldn't get bail for him."

"Then they must have cogent evidence, surely something other than the manifest motive. He has talked, of course?"

"He certainly has."

"He has told of his going to the door of Karnow's room yesterday afternoon?"

"Yes."

"Do you know what time that was?"

"Half-past three. Very close to that."

"Then opportunity is established, and motive. As

for the weapon, the published account says it was Karnow's. Has that been challenged?"

"Not that I know of."

"Then the formula is complete; but a man cannot be convicted by a formula and should not be charged by one. Have they got evidence? Do you know?"

"I know one thing." She was frowning at him, concentrated, intent. "They told Paul that one of his business cards was found in Sidney's pocket—the agency name and address, with his name in the corner—and asked him to account for it. He said he and his salesmen hand out dozens of cards every day, and Sidney could have got one many different places. Then they told him this card had his fingerprints on it—clear, fresh ones—and asked him to account for that."

"Could he?"

"He didn't to them, but he did to me later, when they let me see him."

"How did he account for it?"

She hesitated. "I don't like to, but I have to. He had remembered that last Friday afternoon, when he went to a conference at Jim Beebe's office, he had left one of his cards there on Jim's desk."

"Who was at the conference?"

"Besides Paul—and Jim, of course—there were Sidney's Aunt Margaret—Mrs. Savage—and Dick Savage, and Ann and her husband, Norman Horne."

"Were you there?"

"No. I—I didn't want to go. I had had enough of all the talk."

"You say he left one of his cards on Mr. Beebe's desk. Do you mean he remembers that the card was on the desk when he left the conference?"

"Yes, he's pretty sure it was, but anyway, he left first. All the others were still there."

"Has Mr. Aubry now told the police of this?"

"I don't think so. He thought he wouldn't, because he thought it would look as if he were trying to accuse one of Sidney's relatives, and that would hurt more than it would help. That was why I didn't like to tell you about it, but I knew I had to."

Wolfe grunted. "You did indeed, madam. You are in no position to afford the niceties of decent reticence. Since your husband was almost certainly killed by someone who was mortally inconvenienced by his resurrection, and we are excluding you and Mr. Aubry, his other heirs invite scrutiny and will get it. According to what Mr. Aubry told me yesterday, there are three of them: Mrs. Savage, her son, and her daughter. Where is Mr. Savage?"

"He died years ago. Mrs. Savage is Sidney's mother's sister."

"She got, as did her son and her daughter, nearly a third of a million. What did that sum mean to her? What were her circumstances?"

"I guess it meant a great deal. She wasn't well off."

"What was she living on?"

"Well—Sidney had been helping her."

Wolfe tightened his lips and turned a palm up. "My dear madam. Be as delicate as you please about judgments, but I merely want facts. Must I drag them out of you? A plain question: was Mrs. Savage living on Mr. Karnow's bounty?"

She swallowed. "Yes."

"What has she done with her legacy? Has she conserved it? The fact as you know it."

"No, she hasn't." Caroline's chin lifted a little. "You're quite right, I'm being silly—and anyway, lots of people know all about it. Mrs. Savage bought a house in New York, and last winter she bought a villa in southern France, and she wears expensive clothes and gives big parties. I don't know how much she has left. Dick had a job with a downtown broker, but he quit when he got the inheritance from Sidney, and he is still looking for something to do. He is—well, he likes to be with women. It's hard to be fair to Ann because she has wasted herself. She is beautiful and clever, and she's only twenty-six, but there she is, married to Norman Horne, just throwing herself away."

"What does Mr. Horne do?"

"He tells people about the time twelve years ago when he scored four touchdowns for Yale against Princeton."

"Is that lucrative?"

"No. He says he isn't fitted for a commercial society. I can't stand him, and I don't understand how Ann can. They live in an apartment on Park Avenue, and she pays the rent, and as far as I know she pays everything. She must."

"Well." Wolfe sighed. "So that's the job. While Mr. Aubry's motive was admittedly more powerful than theirs, since he stood to lose not only his fortune but also his wife, they were by no means immune to temptation. How much have you been associating with them the past two years?"

"Not much. With Aunt Margaret and Dick almost not at all. I used to see Ann fairly often, but very little since she married Norman Horne."

"When was that marriage?"

"Two years ago. Soon after the estate was distributed." She stopped, and then decided to go on. "That was one of Ann's unpredictable somersaults. She was engaged to Jim Beebe—announced publicly, and the date set—and then, without even bothering to break it off, she married Norman Horne."

"Was Mr. Horne a friend of your husband's?"

"No, they never met. Ann found Norman—I don't know where. They wouldn't have been friends even if they had met, because Sidney wouldn't have liked him. There weren't many people Sidney did like."

"Did he like his relatives?"

"No—if you want facts. He didn't. He saw very little of them."

"I see." Wolfe leaned back and closed his eyes, and his lips began to work, pushing out and then pulling in, out and in, out and in. He only does that when he has something substantial to churn around in his skull. But that time I thought he was being a little premature, since he hadn't even seen them yet, not one. Caroline started to say something, but I shook my head at her, and she subsided.

Finally Wolfe opened his eyes and spoke. "You understand, madam, that the circumstances—particularly the finding of Mr. Aubry's card, bearing his fingerprints, on the body—warrant an explicit assumption: that your husband was killed by one of the six persons present at the conference in Mr. Beebe's office Friday afternoon; and, eliminating Mr. Aubry, five are left. You know them all, if not intimately at least familiarly, and I ask you: is one of them more likely than another? For any reason at all?"

She shook her head. "I don't know. Do we have to —is this the only way?"

"It is. That's our assumption until it's discredited. I want your best answer."

"I don't know," she insisted.

I decided to contribute. "I doubt," I put in, "if this would be a good buy at a nickel, but this morning at the DA's office I met the whole bunch. I had a little chat with Mrs. Horne, who seems to like gags, and when the others appeared she introduced me to them. She told them I was going to give her the third degree, and she added, I quote, 'I expect I'll go to pieces and confess—' Unquote. At that point Horne put his hand on her mouth and told her she talked too much. Mrs. Savage said it was her sense of humor."

"That's like Ann," Caroline said. "Exactly like her, at her worst."

Wolfe grunted. "Mr. Goodwin has a knack for putting women at their worst. He's no help, and neither are you. You seem not to realize that unless I can expose one of those five as the murderer of your husband, Mr. Aubry is almost certainly doomed."

"I do realize it. It's awful, but I do." Her lips tightened. In a moment she spoke. "And I want to help! All night I was trying to think, and one thing I thought of —what Sidney said in his letter about something that would shock me. You said yesterday it's not simple to disinherit a wife, but couldn't he have done it some other way? Couldn't he have signed something that would give someone a claim on the estate, perhaps the whole thing? Isn't there some way he could have arranged for the—shock?"

"Conceivably," Wolfe admitted. "But there would have had to be an authentic transfer of ownership and possession, and there wasn't. Or if he established a trust it would have had to be legally recorded, and the estate would never have been distributed. You'll have to do better than that." He cleared his throat explosively and straightened up. "Very well. I must tackle them. Will you please have them here at six o'clock, madam? All of them?"

Her eyes widened at him. "Me? Bring them here?"

"Certainly."

"But I can't! How? What could I say? I can't tell

them that you think one of them killed Sidney, and you want—No! I can't!" She came forward in the chair. "Don't you see it's just impossible? Anyhow, they wouldn't come!"

Wolfe turned. "Archie. You'll have to get them. I prefer six o'clock, but if that isn't feasible after dinner will do." He glanced up at the wall clock. "Phone Mr. Parker and make an appointment for Mrs. Karnow. Phone Saul and tell him I want him here as soon as possible. Then lunch. After lunch, proceed." He turned to the client. "Will you join us, madam? Fritz's rice-and-mushroom fritters are, if I may say so, palatable."

IV

Since this is a democracy, thank God, please prepare to vote. All those in favor of my describing in full detail my efforts to the utmost, lasting a good five hours, to fill Wolfe's order for three males and two females, say aye. I hear none. Since my eardrums are sensitive I won't ask for the noes.

Then I'll sketch it. James M. Beebe, I found, was not one of the machines in one of the huge legal factories that occupy so many floors in so many of New York's skyscrapers. He was soloing it in a modest space on the tenth floor of a midtown building. The woman in the little anteroom, the only visible or audible employee, with a typewriter on her left and a telephone on her right, said Mr. Beebe would be back soon, and, if you call thirty-five minutes soon, he was.

The inner room he led me to must have been a little cramped with a conference of six people. Its furniture was adequate but by no means ornate. Beebe, who had looked runty alongside Mrs. Savage, could not be called impressive seated at his desk, with a large percentage of the area of his thin face taken up by the black-rimmed glasses. When I showed him my credentials, a note signed by Caroline Karnow saying that Nero Wolfe was acting for her, and told him that Wolfe would like to discuss the situation with those chiefly concerned at his office that afternoon or evening, he said that he understood that the police investigation was making progress, and that he questioned the wisdom of an investigation of a murder by a private detective.

Wise or not, I said, Mrs. Karnow surely had the right to hire Wolfe if she wanted to. He conceded that. Also surely the widow of his former friend and client might reasonably expect him to cooperate in her effort to discover the truth. Wasn't that so?

He looked uncomfortable. He saw that a pencil on his desk was not in its proper place, and moved it, and studied it a while to decide if that was the best spot after all. At length he came back to me.

"It's like this, Mr. Goodwin," he piped. "I sympathize deeply with Mrs. Karnow, of course. But any obligation I am under is not to her, but to my late friend and client, Sidney Karnow. I certainly will do anything I can to help discover the truth, but it is justifiable to suppose that in employing Nero Wolfe Mrs. Karnow's primary purpose, if not her sole purpose, is to save Paul Aubry. As an officer of the law I cannot conscientiously participate in that. I am not Aubry's attorney. I beg you to understand."

I kept after him. He stood pat. Finally, following instructions from Wolfe, I put a question to him.

"I suppose," I said, "you won't mind helping to clear up a detail. At a conference in this room last Friday afternoon Aubry left one of his business cards on your desk. It was there when he left. What happened to it?"

He cocked his head and frowned. "Here on my desk?"

"Right."

The frown deepened. "I'm trying to remember— yes, I do remember. He suggested I might phone him later, and he put it there."

"What happened to it?"

"I don't know."

"Did you phone him?"

"No. As it turned out, there was no occasion to."

"Would you mind seeing if the card is around? It's fairly important."

"Why is it important?"

"That's a long story. But I would like very much to see that card. Will you take a look?"

He wasn't enthusiastic about it, but he obliged. He looked among and under things on top of his desk, including the blotter, in the desk drawers, and around the room some—as, for instance, on top of a filing cabinet. I got down on my knees to see under the desk. No card.

I scrambled to my feet. "May I ask your secretary?"

"What's this all about?" he demanded.

"Nothing you would care to participate in. But the easiest way to get rid of me is to humor me on this one little detail."

He lifted the phone and spoke to it, and in a moment the door opened and the employee entered. He told her I wanted to ask her something, and I did so. She said she knew nothing about any card of Paul Aubry's. She had never seen one, on Beebe's desk or anywhere else, last Friday or any other day. That settled, she backed out, pulling the door with her.

"It's a little discouraging," I told Beebe. "I was counting on collecting that card. Are you sure you don't remember seeing one of the others pick it up?"

"I've told you all I remember—that Aubry put a card on my desk."

"Was there an opportunity for one of them to pick it up without your noticing?"

"There might have been. I don't know what you're trying to establish, Mr. Goodwin, but I will not be led by you to a commitment, even here privately. Probably during the meeting here on Friday I had occasion to leave this chair to get something from my files. I won't say that gave someone an opportunity to remove something from my desk, but I can't prohibit you from saying so." He got to his feet. "I'm sorry I can't be more helpful."

"So am I," I said emphatically.

I arose and turned to go, but halfway to the door his voice came. "Mr. Goodwin."

I turned. He had left his chair and was standing at the end of the desk, stiff and straight. "I'm a lawyer," he said in a different tone, "but I am also a man. Speaking as a man, I ask you to consider my position. My friend and client has been murdered, and the police are apparently convinced that they have the murderer in custody. Nero Wolfe, acting for Mrs. Karnow, wants to prove them wrong. His only hope of success is to fasten the guilt elsewhere. Isn't that the situation?"

"Roughly, yes."

"And you ask me to cooperate. You mentioned a conference in this office last Friday. Besides myself, there were five people here—you know who they were. None of them was, or is, my client. They were all dismayed by the return of Sidney Karnow alive. They were all in dread of personal financial calamity. They all asked me, one way or another, to intercede for them. I have of course given this information to the police, and I see no impropriety in my giving it also to Nero Wolfe. Beyond that I have absolutely no information or evidence that could possibly help him. I tell you frankly, if Paul Aubry is guilty I hope he is convicted and punished; but if one of the others is guilty I hope he—or she—is punished, and if I knew anything operant to that end I certainly would not withhold it."

He lifted a hand and dropped it. "All I'm trying to say—as a lawyer I'm not supposed to be vindictive, but as a man perhaps I am a little. Whoever killed Sidney Karnow should be punished." He turned and went back to his chair.

"A damn fine sentiment," I agreed, and left him.

On the way to the next customer I found a booth and phoned Wolfe a report. All I got in return was a series of grunts.

The house Mrs. Savage had bought was in the Sixties, over east of Lexington Avenue. I am not an expert on Manhattan real estate, but after a look at the narrow gray brick three-layer item my guess was that it had set her back not more than a tenth of her three hundred thousand, not counting the mortgage. When there was no answer to my rings I felt cheated. I hadn't expected anything as lavish as a dolled-up butler, but not even a maid to receive detectives?

It was only a ten-minute walk to the Park Avenue address of Mr. and Mrs. Norman Horne. My luck stayed stubborn. The hallman said they were both out, phoned up at my request, and got no answer.

I like to walk around Manhattan, catching glimpses of its wild life, the pigeons and cats and girls, but that day I overdid it, back and forth between my two objectives. Finally, from an ambush in a hamburger hell on Sixty-eighth Street, where I was sipping a glass of milk, I saw Aunt Margaret navigate the sidewalk across the street and enter the gray brick. I finished the milk, crossed over, and pushed the button.

She opened the door a few inches, thought she saw a journalist, said, "I have nothing to say," and would have closed the door if it hadn't been for my foot.

"Wait a minute," I objected. "We've been introduced—by your daughter, this morning. The name is Archie Goodwin."

She let the door come another inch for a better view of me, and the pressure of my foot kept it going. I crossed the threshold.

"Of course," she said. "We were rude to you, weren't we? The reason I said I have nothing to say, they tell me that's what I must say to everybody, but it's quite true that my daughter introduced you, and we were rude. What do you want?"

She sounded to me like a godsend. If I could kidnap her and get her down to the office, and phone the rest of them that we had her and she was being very helpful, it was a good bet that they would come on the run to yank her out of our clutches.

I gave her a friendly eye and a warm smile. "I'll tell you, Mrs. Savage. As your daughter told you, I work for Nero Wolfe. He thinks there are some aspects of this situation that haven't been sufficiently considered. To mention only one, there's the legal principle that a criminal may not profit by his crime. If it should be proved that Aubry killed your nephew, and that Mrs. Karnow was an accessory, what happens to her half of the estate? Does it go to you and your son and daughter, or what? That's the sort of thing Mr. Wolfe wants to discuss with you. If you'll come on down to his office with me, he's waiting there for you. He wants to know how you feel about it, and he wants your advice. It will only take us—"

A roar came from above. "What's going on, Mumsy?"

Heavy feet were descending stairs behind Mrs. Savage in a hurry. She turned. "Oh, Dickie? I supposed you were asleep."

He was in a silk dressing gown that must have accounted for at least two Cs of Cousin Sidney's dough. I could have choked him. He had been there all the time. After ignoring all my bell ringing for the past two hours, here he was horning in just when I was getting a good start on a snatch.

"You remember Mr. Goodwin," his mother was telling him. "Down at that place this morning? He wants to take me to see Nero Wolfe. Mr. Wolfe wants to ask my advice about a very interesting point. I think I should go, I really do."

"I don't," Dick said bluntly.

"But Dickie," she appealed, "I'm sure you agree that we should do all we can to get this awful business over and done with!"

"Sure I do," he conceded. "God knows I do. But how it could help for you to go and discuss it with a private detective—No, I don't see it."

They looked at each other. The mutual resemblance was so remarkable that you might say they had the same face, allowing for the difference in age; and also they were built alike. Her bulk was more bone and meat than fat, and so was his.

When she spoke I got a suspicion that I had misjudged her. Her tone was new, dry and cool and meaningful. "I think I ought to go," she said.

He appealed now. "Please, Mumsy. At least we can talk it over. You can go later, after dinner." He turned to me. "Could she see Wolfe this evening?"

"She could," I admitted. "Now would be better."

"I really am tired," she told me. Her tone was back to what might have been normal. "All this awful business. After dinner would be better. What is the address?"

I got my wallet, took out a card, and handed it to her. "By the way," I observed, "that reminds me. At that meeting last Friday at Mr. Beebe's office, Aubry put one of his cards on Beebe's desk and left it there. Do you happen to remember what became of it?"

Mrs. Savage said promptly, "I remember he took out a card, but I don't—"

"Hold it," Dick barked at her, gripping her arm so hard that she winced. "Go upstairs."

She tried to twist loose, found it wouldn't work, and leveled her eyes at him to stare him off. That didn't work either. His eyes were as level as hers, and harder and meaner. Four seconds of it was enough for her. When he turned her around she didn't resist, and without a word she walked to the stairs and started up. He faced me and demanded, "What's this about a card?"

"What I said. Aubry put one on Beebe's desk—"

"Who says he did?"

"Aubry."

"Yeah? A guy in for murder? Come again."

"Glad to. Beebe says so too."

Dick snorted. "That little louse? That punk?" He lifted a hand to tap my chest with a finger, but a short backward step took me out of range. "Listen, brother. If you and your boss think you can frame an out for Aubry don't let me stop you, but don't come trying to work my mother in, or me either. Is that plain?"

"I merely want to know—"

"The way out," he said rudely, and strode to the door and opened it. Since I stay where I'm not wanted only when there is a chance of gaining something, I took advantage of his courtesy and passed on through to the sidewalk.

I was getting low on prospects. Back at the Park Avenue address, where the hallman and I were by now on intimate terms, he informed me that Mrs. Horne had come in, and he had told her that Mr. Goodwin had called several times and would return, and she had said to send me up.

At Apartment D on the twelfth floor I was admitted by a maid, properly outfitted, who showed me to a living room where a slice of Karnow's money had been used with no great taste but a keen eye to comfort. I sat down, and almost at once got up again when Ann Horne entered. She met me and let me have a hand.

"We'll have to hurry," she said. "My husband may be home any minute. What do you do first, rubber hose?"

She was wearing a nice simple blue dress that either was silk or wanted to be, and had renovated her make-up since coming in from the street.

"Not here," I told her. "Get the stole. I'm taking you to a dungeon."

She flowed onto a couch. "Sit down and describe it to me. Rats, I hope?"

"No, we can't get rats to stay. Bad air." I sat. "As a matter of fact, I've decided the physical approach wouldn't work with you, and we're going after you mentally. That's Mr. Wolfe's department, and he never leaves the house, so I've come to take you down there. You can leave word for your husband, and he can join us."

"That doesn't appeal to me at all. Mentally I'm a wreck already. What's the matter, are you afraid I can't take it?"

"On the contrary, I'm afraid I can't give it. Nature went to a lot of trouble with you, and I'd hate to spoil it. You'd enjoy a session with Nero Wolfe. He's afraid of women anyhow, and you'd scare him stiff."

She pulled a routine that I approved of. Knowing that if she took a cigarette I'd have to get up to light it, she first picked up a lighter and flicked it on, and then reached to a box for the cigarette. A darned good idea.

"What's the score?" she asked, after inhaling and letting it out.

I told her. "Paul Aubry is charged with murder. Mr. Wolfe can earn a big fee only by clearing him. Mr. Wolfe has never let a big fee get away. So Aubry will be cleared. We'll be glad to let you share the glory, though not the fee. Get the stole, and let's go."

"You're irresistible," she said admiringly. "It's too bad about Paul."

"Not at all. When he gets out he can marry his wife."

"*If* he gets out. Do you remember nursery rhymes?"

"I wrote them."

"Then of course you remember this one:

> "Needles and pins,
> Needles and pins,
> When a man murders
> His trouble begins."

"Sure, that's one of my favorites. Only Aubry didn't murder."

She nodded. "That's your line, of course, and you're

stuck with it." She reached to crush her cigarette in a tray, then suddenly turned to me with her eyes flashing. "All this poppycock! All this twaddle about life being sacred! For everybody there's just one life that's sacred, and everybody knows it! Mine!" She spread her hand on her breast. "Mine! And Sidney's was sacred to him, but he's dead. So it's too bad about Paul."

"If you feel that way about it you ought to be ready to give him a lift."

"I might be if I had anything to lift with."

"Maybe I can furnish something. Last Friday you were at a conference at Jim Beebe's office. Aubry put one of his business cards on Beebe's desk. Why did you pick up that card, and what did you do with it?"

She stared at me a moment. Then she shook her head. "You'll have to get out the rubber hose, or pliers to pull out my nails. Even then I may hold out."

"Didn't you pick up the card?"

"I did not."

"Then who did?"

"I have no idea—if there was a card."

"You don't remember Aubry putting it on the desk? Or seeing it there?"

"No. But this begins to sound like something. You sound as if you're really detecting. Are you?"

I nodded. "This is called the double sly squeeze. First I get you to deny you touched the card, which I have done. Then I display one of Aubry's cards in a cellophane envelope, tell you it has fingerprints on it which I suspect are yours, and dare you to let me take your prints so I can check. You're afraid to refuse—"

"Come and show me how you take my prints. I've never had it done."

I was, I admit it, curious. Was she inviting physical contact because she was like that, or was she expecting to voodoo me, or was she merely passing the time? To find out I got up and went to her, took her offered hand and got it snugly in mine, palm up, and bent over it for a closeup. The hand seemed to be telling me that it didn't mind the operation at all, and with the fingertips of my other hand I spread her fingers apart, bending lower.

Of course I was concentrated on the job. Whether the door from the outside hall to the foyer was opened so quietly that no sound came, or whether my ears caught a sound but I ignored it, what interrupted my investigation was her sudden tight grip on my hand as she straightened up and cried, "Don't! You're hurting me! Norman—thank God!"

My whirl around was checked for a second by her hold on my hand. For her size and sex she had muscle. I suppose to Norman Horne, approaching from behind me, it could have looked as if I were holding her, instead of her me, but even so it must have been obvious that I was turning, and he might have held his fire until I could at least see it coming. As it was, I was off balance when he plugged me on the side of the jaw, and I went clear down, sprawling. Added to the four touchdowns he had scored for Yale against Princeton, that made five.

"He was trying to force me—" Ann was saying with her sense of humor.

Probably I would have scrambled to my feet and departed, since Wolfe wouldn't have appreciated my letting my personal feelings take charge when I was on a job, if it hadn't been for Horne's attitude. He was glaring down at me, with his fists ready, and it was doubtful if he would wait till I got farther up than on my knees. So I did a quick double roll, sprang all the way up, and faced him. He came at me wide open, as if

I had been a dummy, and swung. There wouldn't have been the slightest excuse for my missing the exact spot for a dead kidney punch, and I didn't. Air exploded out of him, and he crumpled, not sprawling, but in a compact heap. Then he sort of settled to get comfortable.

His attractive wife took a couple of steps toward him, stopped to look at me, and said, "I'll be damned."

"You will if they consult me," I told her emphatically, turned, went to the foyer and got my hat, and let myself out. On the way down in the elevator I felt my jaw and took a look at it in the mirror, and decided I would live.

I got home just at the dinner hour, seven-thirty, and since it takes an earthquake to postpone a meal in that house, and no mention of business is permitted at the table, my full report of the afternoon had to wait. If the main dish had been something like goulash or calves' brains probably nothing unusual in my technique would have been apparent, but it was squabs, which of course have to be gnawed off the bones, and while I was working on the second one Wolfe demanded, "What the deuce is the matter with you?"

"Nothing. What?"

"You're not eating, you're nibbling."

"Yeah. Broken jaw. With the compliments of Ann Horne."

He stared. "A *woman* broke your jaw?"

"Sorry, no shoptalk at meals. I'll tell you later."

I did so, in the office, after dinner, and after I had looked into a little matter I was wondering about. I had obeyed the instruction, given me before lunch, to phone Saul Panzer, and Saul had said he would be at the office at two-thirty. By that time I had left. When, on the way from the dining room to the office, I asked

Wolfe if Saul had come, he replied in one word, "Yes," indicating that that was all I needed to know about it. Thinking it wouldn't hurt me any to know more, I went and opened the safe and got out the little book from the cash drawer. Sometimes, in addition to the name and date and amount, Wolfe scribbles something about the purpose, but that time he hadn't. The latest entry was merely the date and "SP $1000." All that did was make me wonder further what Saul was expected to buy that might cost as much as a grand.

As I reported on my afternoon rounds, giving all conversations verbatim, which isn't so hard when you've had plenty of practice and have learned that nothing less will be acceptable, Wolfe leaned back in his chair with his eyes closed. He was too damn placid. Ordinarily, when he sends me out for bacon and I return empty-handed, he makes some pointed cracks, no matter how hopeless he knows my errand was; but that time, not a one. That meant either that he didn't like the job and to hell with it, or that I was just a sideshow, including my sore jaw, and the main attraction was elsewhere. When I was through he didn't open his eyes or ask a single question.

I groaned with pain. "Since it's obvious that I wasted five hours of your time, and since if I stay here I may say something that will rile you, I guess I'll go see Doc Vollmer and have him set my jaw. He'll probably have to wire it."

"No."

"No what?"

He opened his eyes. "I'm expecting a phone call. Probably not until tomorrow, but it could come this evening. If it does I'll need you."

"Okay, I'll be upstairs."

I mounted the two flights to my room, turned on

the lights, went to the bathroom mirror to see if there was enough swelling for a compress, decided there wasn't, and settled myself in my easy chair with a collection of magazines.

Nearly two hours had gone by, and I was yawning, when a sound came faintly through the open door—the sound of Wolfe's voice. I went and lifted the phone on my bedside table and put it to my ear. It was dead. I had neglected to plug it in when I left the office. It would have been undignified to go to the hall, to the stair landing, and listen, so I did; but though Wolfe's voice came up at intervals I couldn't get the words. After enough of that I returned to the room and the easy chair, but had barely lowered myself into it when a bellow from below came.

"Archie! *Archie!*"

I did not descend the stairs three steps at a time, but I admit I didn't mosey. Wolfe, at his desk, spoke as I entered the office. "Get Mr. Cramer."

Getting Inspector Cramer of Homicide, day or night, may be very simple or it may be impossible. That time it was in between. He was at his office on Twentieth Street, but in conference and not available, so I had to bear down and make it plain that if he didn't speak with Nero Wolfe immediately God only knew what tomorrow's papers would say.

In a couple of minutes his familiar growl was growling at me. "Goodwin? Is Wolfe on?"

I nodded at Wolfe, and he took up his phone. "Mr. Cramer? I don't know if you know that I'm investigating the Karnow murder. For a client. Mrs. Karnow engaged me at noon today."

"Go ahead and investigate. What do you want?"

"I understand that Mr. Aubry is being held on a murder charge, without bail. That's regrettable, because he's innocent. If you are supporting that charge I advise you to reconsider. On the soundness of that advice I stake my professional reputation."

I would have paid admission to see Cramer's face. He knew Wolfe would rather go without eating a whole day than be caught wrong in a flat statement like that.

"That's all I wanted, your advice." The growl was still a growl, but not the same. "Is it all right if I wait till morning to turn him loose?"

"Formalities may require it. May I ask a question? How many of the others—Mrs. Savage, her son, Mr. and Mrs. Horne, Mr. Beebe—have been eliminated by alibis?"

"Crossed off, no one. But Aubry not only has no alibi, he admits he was there."

"Yes, I know. However, it was one of the others. I must now choose between alternatives. Either I proceed independently to disclose and hand over the culprit, or I invite you to partake. Which would you prefer?"

It was nearly silence, but I thought I could hear Cramer breathe. "Are you saying you've got it?"

"I'm saying I am prepared to expose the murderer. It would be a little simpler if you can spare the time, for I must have them here at my office, and for you that will be no problem. If you care to take part could you get them here in half an hour?"

Cramer cussed. Since it's a misdemeanor to use profanity over the phone, and since I don't want to hang a misdemeanor rap on an inspector, I won't quote it. He added, "I'm coming up there. I'll be there in five minutes."

"You won't get in." Wolfe wasn't nasty, but he was firm. "If you come without those people, or without

first assuring me that they will be brought, Mr. Goodwin won't even open the door to the crack the chain
bolt will permit. He's in a touchy mood because a man
hit him on the jaw and knocked him down. Nor am I in
any humor to wrangle with you. I gave you your
chance. Do you remember that when you were here
this morning I told you that I had the last letter Mrs.
Karnow received from her husband, and offered to
show it to you?"

"Yes."

"And you said you weren't interested in a letter
Karnow wrote nearly three years ago. You were
wrong. I now offer again to show it to you before I
send it to the District Attorney, but only on the condition as stated. Well?"

I'll say one thing for Cramer, he knew when he was
out of choices, and he didn't try to prolong it. He
cussed again and then got it out. "They'll be there, and
so will I."

Wolfe hung up. I asked him, "What about our client? Hadn't she better be present?"

He made a face. "I suppose so. See if you can get
her."

V

It was half-past eleven when I ushered Norman
Horne and his attractive wife to the office and to the
two vacant seats in the cluster of chairs that had been
placed facing Wolfe's desk. At their left was Mrs. Savage; behind them were Dick Savage, James M. Beebe,
and Sergeant Purley Stebbins—only not in that order,
because Purley was in the middle, behind Ann Horne.
There had been another chair in the cluster, for Caro-

line Karnow, but she had moved it away, over to the side of the room where the bookshelves were, while I was in the hall admitting Mrs. Savage and Dick. That had put her where Purley couldn't see her without turning his head a full quarter-circle, and he hadn't liked it, but I had let him know that it was none of his damn business where our client sat.

The red leather chair was for Cramer, who was in the dining room with Wolfe. After the Hornes had greeted their relatives, including Caroline, and got seated, I crossed to the dining room and told Wolfe we were ready, and he marched to the office and to his desk, and stood.

"Archie?"

"Yes, sir." I was there. "Front row, from the left, Mr. Horne, Mrs. Horne, Mrs. Savage. Rear, from the left, Mr. Savage, Mr. Stebbins you know, and Mr. Beebe."

Wolfe nodded almost perceptibly, sat, and turned his head. "Mr. Cramer?"

Cramer, standing, was surveying them. "I can't say this is unofficial," he conceded, "since I asked you to come here, and I'm here. But anything Mr. Wolfe says to you is solely on his own responsibility, and you're under no obligation to answer any questions he asks if you don't want to. I want that clearly understood."

"Even so," Beebe piped up, "isn't this rather irregular?"

"If you mean unusual, yes. If you mean improper, I don't think so. You weren't ordered to come, you were asked, and you're here. Do you want to leave?"

Apparently they didn't, at least not enough to make an issue of it. They exchanged glances, and someone muttered something. Beebe said, "We certainly reserve the right to leave."

"Nobody will stop you," Cramer assured him, and sat. He looked at Wolfe. "Go ahead."

Wolfe adjusted himself in his chair to achieve the maximum of comfort, and then moved his eyes, left and right, to take them in. He spoke. "Mr. Cramer assured you that you are not obliged to answer my questions. I can relieve your minds of that concern. I doubt if I'll have a single question to put to any of you, though of course an occasion for one may arise. I merely want to describe the situation as it now stands and invite your comment. You may have none."

He interlaced his fingers at the crest of his central bulge. "The news that Mr. Karnow had been murdered was brought here by Mr. Stebbins early last evening, but my interest in it was only casual until Mrs. Karnow came at noon today and aroused it by hiring me. Then I gave it my attention, and it seemed to me that your obvious motive for murder—Mrs. Savage and her son and daughter, and Mr. Horne as the daughter's husband—was not very compelling. From what my client told me of Mr. Karnow's character and temperament, it seemed unlikely that any of you would so fear harsh and exigent demands from him that you would be driven to the dangerous and desperate act of murder. You had received your legacies legally and properly, in good faith, and surely you would at least have first tried an appeal to his reason and his grace. So one of you must have had a stronger motive."

Wolfe cleared his throat. "That derogation of your obvious motives put me up a stump. There were two people with overpowering motives: Mr. Aubry and Mrs. Karnow. Not only did they stand to forfeit a much larger sum than any of you, but also they faced a deprivation even more intolerable. He would lose her, and she would lose him. It is not surprising that Mr.

Cramer and his colleagues were dazzled by the glitter of that powerful motive. I might have been similarly bemused but for two circumstances. The first was that I had concluded that neither Mrs. Karnow nor Mr. Aubry had committed murder. If they had, they had come fresh from that ferocious deed to engage me to negotiate for them with the man one of them had just killed, for the devious purpose of raising the presumption that they didn't know he was dead, and I had sat here and conversed with them for an hour without feeling any twinge of suspicion that they were diddling me. I was compelled either to reject that notion or abandon certain pretensions that feed my ego. The choice wasn't difficult."

"Also Mrs. Karnow was your client," Cramer said pointedly.

Wolfe ignored it, which was just as well. He went on. "The second circumstance was that the possibility of another motive had been suggested to me. It was suggested in a letter which Mrs. Karnow had shown me yesterday—the last letter she had received from her husband, nearly three years ago." He opened a drawer and took out sheets of paper. "Here it is. I'll read only the pertinent excerpt:

"Speaking of death, if he should get me instead of me getting him, something I did before I left New York will give you quite a shock. I wish I could be around to see how you take it. You claim you have never worried about money, that it's not worth it. Also you've told me that I always talk sardonic but haven't got it in me to act sardonic. This will show you. I'll admit I have to die to get the last laugh, but that will be sardonic too. I wonder do I love you or hate you? They're hard to tell apart. Remember me in thy dreams."

He returned the papers to the drawer and closed it. "Mrs. Karnow had the notion that what her husband had done was to make a new will, leaving her out, but that theory was open to two objections. First, a wife cannot be so brusquely disinherited by a man of means; and second, such an act would have been merely malicious, not sardonic. But the phrase 'speaking of death' did imply some connection with his will, and raised the question, how might such a man have so remade his will as to cause such a woman to worry about money? That intention was clearly implied."

Wolfe turned a hand over. "Under the circumstances as I knew them, a plausible conjecture offered itself: that Karnow had made a new will, leaving everything to his wife. That would certainly give her an inescapable worry about money, the same worry he had had—how much should his relatives be pampered? And since it was his money and they were his relatives, for her the worry would be even more bothersome than for him. I would call that sardonic. Also he might have been moved by another consideration, a reluctance to bestow large amounts on them. I had gathered, though Mrs. Karnow didn't make it explicit, that in matters of personal finance and economy Karnow did not regard his relatives as paragons—a judgment that has been verified by their management of their bequests."

Ann Horne's head jerked around, and she told Caroline, "Thank you so much, Lina darling." Caroline made no reply. Judging from her intent face and rigid posture, if she replied to anything it would be an explosion.

"Therefore," Wolfe resumed, "it appeared that the hypothesis that Karnow had made a new will deserved a little exploration. To ask any of you about it would of course have been jackassery. It was reasonable to suppose that for such a chore he would have called upon his friend and attorney, Mr. Beebe, but it seemed impolitic to approach Mr. Beebe on the matter. I don't know whether any of you has ever heard the name Saul Panzer?"

No reply. No shake of a head. They might all have been in a trance.

"I employ Mr. Panzer," Wolfe said, "on important missions for which Mr. Goodwin cannot be spared. He has extraordinary qualities and abilities. I told him that if Mr. Beebe had drafted a new will for Mr. Karnow it had probably been typed by his secretary, and Mr. Panzer undertook to see Mr. Beebe's secretary and try to get on terms with her without arousing her suspicion. I would entrust so ticklish an errand to no other man except Mr. Goodwin. Early this afternoon he called on her in the guise of an invesigator from the Federal Security Agency, wanting to clear up some confusion about her Social Security number."

"Impersonating an officer of the law," Beebe protested.

"Possibly," Wolfe conceded. "If such an investigator is an officer of the law, he is a federal officer, and Mr. Panzer can await his doom. In ten minutes he collected an arsenal of data. Mr. Beebe's secretary, whose name is Vera O'Brien, has been with him two and one-half years. Her predecessor, whose name was Helen Martin, left Mr. Beebe's employ in November nineteen-fifty-one to marry a man named Arthur Rabson, and went to live with her husband in Florence, South Carolina, where he owns a garage. So if Karnow made a new will before he left New York, and if Mr. Beebe drafted it, and if Mr. Beebe's secretary typed it, it was typed by the now Mrs. Arthur Rabson."

"Three ifs," Cramer muttered.

"Yes," Wolfe agreed, "but open for test. I was tempted to get Mrs. Rabson on the phone in South Carolina, but it was too risky, so Mr. Panzer took a plane to Columbia, and I phoned there and chartered a small one to take him on to Florence. An hour ago, or a little more, I got a phone call from him. He has talked with Mrs. Rabson, she has signed a statement, and she is willing to come to New York if necessary. She says that Mr. Beebe dictated to her a new will for Mr. Karnow in the fall of 1951, that she typed it, and that she was one of the witnesses to Karnow's signature. The other witness was a woman named Nora Wayne, from a nearby office. She supposes that Miss Wayne did not know the contents of the will. By it Karnow left everything to his wife, and it contained a request that she use discretion in making provision for Karnow's relatives, who were named. Mrs. Rabson didn't know that—"

"Sidney wouldn't do that!" Aunt Margaret cried. "I don't believe it! Jim, are you going to just sit there and blink?"

All eyes were at Beebe except Wolfe's. His were on the move. "I should explain," he said, "that meanwhile Mr. Goodwin was making himself useful. He learned, for instance, that the only item of tangible evidence against Mr. Aubry, a card of his that was found in Mr. Karnow's pocket, had been accessible to all of you last Friday in Mr. Beebe's office."

"How's that?" Cramer demanded.

"You'll get it," Wolfe assured him, "and you'll like it." He focused on Beebe. "The occasion has arisen, I think, Mr. Beebe, for a question. As Mr. Cramer told you, you're not obliged to answer it. What happened to Mr. Karnow's last will?"

Thinking it over later, I decided that Beebe probably took his best bet. Him being a lawyer, you might suppose that he would simply have clammed up, but, knowing as he did that he was absolutely hooked on the will, he undoubtedly figured, in the short time he had for figuring, that the best way was to go ahead and take the little one so as to dodge the big one.

He addressed Cramer. "I would like to speak to you privately, Inspector—you and Mr. Wolfe, if you want him present."

Cramer glanced at Wolfe. Wolfe said, "No. You may refuse to answer, or you may answer here and now."

"Very well." Beebe straightened his shoulders and lifted his chin. At the angle I had on him I couldn't see his eyes behind the black-rimmed glasses. "This will ruin me professionally, and I bitterly regret the part I have played. It was a month or so before the notice came that Sidney had been killed in action that I told Ann about the new will he had made. That was my first mistake. I did it because I—of the way I felt about her. At that time I would have done just about anything she wanted. When word came that Sidney had been killed she came to my office and insisted on my showing her the will. I was even—"

"Watch it, Jim!" Ann, turned in her chair, called to him. "You dirty little liar! Ad libbing it, you'll get all twisted—"

"Mrs. Horne!" Wolfe said sharply. "Would you rather hear him or be taken from the room?"

She stayed turned to Beebe. "Go on, Jim, but watch it."

Beebe resumed, "I was then even more infatuated

with her than before. I got the will from the safe and showed it to her, and she took it and stuffed it inside her dress. She insisted on taking it to show to her mother. It's easy to say I should have gone to any length to prevent that—it's easy now, but then I was incapable of opposing her. She took the will with her, and I never saw it again. Two weeks later our engagement was publicly announced. I presented Sidney's former will for probate, and that was completely insane, since I only had Ann's word for it that the new will had been destroyed—even though the girl who had typed the new will had got married and gone away."

Beebe lifted a hand to adjust his cheaters. "I won't say what it was that cured me of my infatuation for Ann Savage. It was—a personal thing, and it was enough to cure me good. I only wish to God it had happened sooner. Of course I couldn't stop the probate of the will without ruining myself. In May the estate was distributed, and later that month Ann married Norman Horne. That ended that business, I thought. I had had my lesson, and it had been a tough one."

He pulled his narrow shoulders back. "Then, two years later, this jolt came. Sidney was alive and would soon be in New York. You can imagine how it hit me, or maybe you can't. I finally got it in focus enough to see that I had only two choices: either fall out of my office window or tell Sidney exactly how it had happened. Meanwhile I had to go through all the motions of talking it over with them and listening to all their crazy suggestions. It wasn't until Monday, day before yesterday, that I decided, and I phoned Ann the next morning, yesterday, that I was going to see Sidney that evening and tell him the whole story. Then came the news that Sidney had been murdered. I don't know who killed him. All I know is what I'm telling you, and of course for me that's enough." He stopped for his mouth to do little spasms. He tagged it. "As a counselor-at-law, I'm through."

I was a little disappointed at Norman Horne. Surely he might have been expected to react manfully and promptly to such an indictment of his attractive wife, but he wasn't even looking at Beebe. He was looking at her, there beside him, and it was not a gaze of loyal and trusting faith. It was just as well that she didn't see it.

She didn't see it because her eyes were on Wolfe. "Is he through?" she asked.

"Apparently, madam, yes. At least for the moment. Would you like to comment?"

"I don't want to make a speech. I don't think I need to. Just that he's a liar. Just lies."

Wolfe shook his head. "I doubt if that's adequate. It wasn't all lies, you know. Mr. Karnow did make a new will; you and Mr. Beebe were engaged to marry but didn't; the estate was distributed under the terms of a previous will, with you as a legatee; and Mr. Karnow did return alive and was murdered. I strongly advise you either to keep silent, even though that would expose you to an adverse presumption, or to tell the truth without reservation. You warned Mr. Beebe of the hazard of an improvised complex lie. I urge you to heed your own warning. Now?"

She glanced aside at her husband, but he had focused on Wolfe. Her head swiveled for a glance to her left, at her mother, but that wasn't met either. She looked at Wolfe. "You're quite a performer, aren't you?"

"Yes," he said.

"I believe you already know the truth."

"If so, for you to try to withhold it would be pointless."

"Well, I'd hate to be pointless. You're right, some of what Jim said was true. He did tell me about the new will, but after the news came that Sidney had been killed in action, not before. He did take it from his safe and let me read it. It did leave everything to Caroline. He said that no one knew its contents except his former secretary, and she had got married and gone to some little town in the South, so she was out of the way. He said there was no other copy of it, and that he was sure Caroline didn't know about it because of a letter she had shown him from Sidney. He said he would destroy it, and I and my mother and brother would inherit under the previous will, if I would marry him. Do you want to know everything we said?"

"I think just the essential points."

"Then I don't need to tell how I really felt about marrying him. I didn't tell him. I agreed to it. I suppose you don't care what I thought, but Sidney was dead, and I thought it was only fair for us to get a share. So I agreed, but I never had any intention of marrying Jim Beebe. He wanted an immediate wedding, before he presented the will for probate, but I talked him out of that, and our engagement was announced. When the will had gone through and the estate had been distributed and we had our share, I married Norman Horne. I didn't know whether Jim had destroyed the new will or not, but that didn't matter because he wouldn't dare to produce it then." She fluttered a hand. "That's all."

"Not quite," Wolfe objected. "The sequel. Mr. Karnow's return."

"Oh, yes." Her tone implied that it was careless of her to overlook that little detail. "Of course Jim killed him. If you mean how I felt about Sidney's turning up alive, you may not believe it, but in a way I was glad of it, because I always liked him. I was sorry for Caroline and Paul, because I liked them too, but I knew Sidney wouldn't try to get our share back from us. There was just one person who didn't dare to face him. Of course Jim did face him when he went to his hotel room, but he wasn't facing him when he killed him—he shot him in the back of the head." She turned to Beebe. "Did you tell him about the will, Jim? I'll bet you didn't. I'll bet he never knew." She turned back to Wolfe. "Will that do for the truth?"

"It'll do for a malicious lie," Beebe squeaked.

Wolfe addressed the law. "I would prefer, Mr. Cramer, to turn the issue of veracity over to you. In my opinion, Mr. Beebe fumbled it, and Mrs. Horne didn't."

At a later date, in a courtroom, a jury concurred. Justice is a fine thing, but that night in Wolfe's office it slipped up on one detail. After Cramer and Stebbins had escorted Beebe out, and the others had gone, Caroline Karnow decided that the occasion called for her returning the kiss she had received in that room twelve hours earlier. But she went right past me, around to Wolfe behind his desk, put her arms around his neck, and gave it to him on both cheeks.

"Wrong address," I said bitterly.

Die
Like a Dog

I

I do sometimes treat myself to a walk in the rain, though I prefer sunshine when there's not enough wind to give the dust a whirl. That rainy Wednesday, however, there was a special inducement: I wanted his raincoat to be good and wet when I delivered it. So with it on my back and my old brown felt on my head, I left the house and set out for Arbor Street, some two miles south in the Village.

Halfway there the rain stopped and my blood had pumped me warm, so I took the coat off, folded it wet side in, hung it on my arm, and proceeded. Arbor Street, narrow and only three blocks long, had on either side an assortment of old brick houses, mostly of four stories, which were neither spick nor span. Number 29 would be about the middle of the first block.

I reached it, but I didn't enter it. There was a party going on in the middle of the block. A police car was double-parked in front of the entrance to one of the houses, and a uniformed cop was on the sidewalk in an attitude of authority toward a small gathering of citizens confronting him. As I approached I heard him demanding, "Whose dog is this?"—referring, evidently, to an animal with a wet black coat standing behind him. I heard no one claim the dog, but I wouldn't have anyway, because my attention was diverted. Another police car rolled up and stopped behind the first one, and a man got out, pushed through the crowd to the sidewalk, nodded to the cop without halting, and went in the entrance, above which appeared the number 29.

The trouble was, I knew the man, which is an understatement. I do not begin to tremble at the sight of Sergeant Purley Stebbins of Manhattan Homicide West, which is also an understatement, but his presence and manner made it a cinch that there was a corpse in that house, and if I demanded entry on the ground that I wanted to swap raincoats with a guy who had walked off with mine, there was no question what would happen. My prompt appearance at the scene of a homicide would arouse all of Purley's worst instincts, backed up by reference to various precedents, and I might not get home in time for dinner, which was going to be featured by grilled squab with a brown sauce which Fritz calls *Vénitienne* and is one of his best.

Purley had disappeared within without spotting me. The cop was a complete stranger. As I slowed down to detour past him on the narrow sidewalk he gave me an eye and demanded, "That your dog?"

The dog was nuzzling my knee, and I stooped to give him a pat on his wet black head. Then, telling the cop he wasn't mine, I went on by. At the next corner I turned right, heading back uptown. I kept my eye peeled for a taxi the first couple of blocks, saw none, and decided to finish the walk. A wind had started in from the west, but everything was still damp from the rain.

Marching along, I was well on my way before I saw the dog. Stopping for a light on Ninth Avenue in the Twenties, I felt something at my knee, and there he was. My hand started for his head in reflex, but I pulled it back. I was in a fix. Apparently he had picked me for a pal, and if I just went on he would follow, and you can't chase a dog on Ninth Avenue by throwing rocks. I could have ditched him by taking a taxi the rest of the way, but that would have been pretty rude after the appreciation he had shown of my charm. He had a collar on with a tag, and could be identified, and the station house was only a few blocks away, so the simplest and cheapest way was to convoy him there. I moved to the curb to look for a taxi coming downtown, and as I did so a cyclone sailed around the corner and took my hat with it into the middle of the avenue.

I didn't dash out into the traffic, but you should have seen that dog. He sprang across the bow of a big truck, wiping its left front fender with his tail, braked landing to let a car by, sprang again, and was under another car—or I thought he was—and then I saw him on the opposite sidewalk. He snatched the hat from under the feet of a pedestrian, turned on a dime, and started back. This time his crossing wasn't so spectacular, but he didn't dally. He came to me and stood, lifting his head and wagging his tail. I took the hat. It had skimmed a puddle of water on its trip, but I thought he would be disappointed if I didn't put it on, so I did. Naturally that settled it. I flagged a cab, took the dog in with me, and gave the driver the address of Wolfe's house.

My idea was to take my hat hound upstairs to my room, give him some refreshment, and phone the

ASPCA to send for him. But there was no sense in passing up such an opportunity for a little buzz at Wolfe, so after letting us in and leaving my hat and the raincoat on the rack in the hall, I proceeded to the door to the office and entered.

"Where the devil have you been?" Wolfe asked grumpily. "We were going over some lists at six o'clock, and it's a quarter to seven."

He was in his oversized chair behind his desk with a book, and his eyes hadn't left the page to spare me a glance. I answered him. "Taking that damn raincoat. Only I didn't deliver it, because—"

"What's that?" he snapped. He was glaring at my companion.

"A dog."

"I see it is. I'm in no temper for buffoonery. Get it out of here."

"Yes, sir, right away. I can keep him in my room most of the time, but of course he'll have to come downstairs and through the hall when I take him out. He's a hat hound. There is a sort of a problem. His name is Nero, which, as you know, means 'black,' and of course I'll have to change it. Ebony would do, or Jet, or Inky, or—"

"Bah. Flummery!"

"No, sir. I get pretty darned lonesome around here, especially during the four hours a day you're up in the plant rooms. You have your orchids, and Fritz has his turtle, and Theodore has his parakeets up in the potting room, and why shouldn't I have a dog? I admit I'll have to change his name, though he is registered as Champion Nero Charcoal of Bantyscoot. I have suggested . . ."

I went on talking only because I had to. It was a fizzle. I had expected to induce a major outburst, even possibly something as frantic as Wolfe leaving his chair to evict the beast himself, and there he was gazing at Nero with an expression I had never seen him aim at any human, including me. I went on talking, forcing it.

He broke in. "It's not a hound. It's a Labrador retriever."

That didn't faze me. I'm never surprised at a display of knowledge by a bird who reads as many books as Wolfe does. "Yes, sir," I agreed. "I only said hound because it would be natural for a private detective to have a hound."

"Labradors," he said, "have a wider skull than any other dog, for brain room. A dog I had when I was a boy, in Montenegro, a small brown mongrel, had a rather narrow skull, but I did not regard it as a defect. I do not remember that I considered that dog to have a defect. Today I suppose I would be more critical. When you smuggled that creature in here did you take into account the disruption it would cause in this household?"

It had backfired on me. I had learned something new about the big fat genius: he would enjoy having a dog around, provided he could blame it on me and so be free to beef when he felt like it. As for me, when I retire to the country I'll have a dog, and maybe two, but not in town.

I snapped into reverse. "I guess I didn't," I confessed. "I do feel the need for a personal pet, but what the hell, I can try a canary or a chameleon. Okay, I'll get rid of him. After all, it's your house."

"I do not want to feel responsible," he said stiffly, "for your privation. I would almost rather put up with its presence than with your reproaches."

"Forget it." I waved a hand. "I'll try to. I promise not to rub it in."

"Another thing," he persisted. "I refuse to interfere with any commitment you have made."

"I have made no commitment."

"Then where did you get it?"

"Well, I'll tell you."

I went and sat at my desk and did so. Nero, the four-legged one, came and lay at my feet with his nose just not touching the toe of my shoe. I reported the whole event, with as much detail as if I had been reporting a vital operation in a major case, and, when I had finished, Wolfe was of course quite aware that my presentation of Nero as a permanent addition to the staff had been a plant. Ordinarily he would have made his opinion of my performance clear, but this time he skipped it, and it was easy to see why. The idea of having a dog that he could blame on me had got in and stuck.

When I came to the end and stopped there was a moment's silence, and then he said, "Jet would be an acceptable name for that dog."

"Yeah." I swiveled and reached for the phone. "I'll call the ASPCA to come for him."

"No." He was emphatic.

"Why not?"

"Because there is a better alternative. Call someone you know in the Police Department—anyone. Give him the number on the dog's tag, and ask him to find out who the owner is. Then you can inform the owner directly."

He was playing for time. It could happen that the owner was dead or in jail or didn't want the dog back, and if so Wolfe could take the position that I had committed myself by bringing the dog home in a taxi and that it would be dishonorable to renege. However, I didn't want to argue, so I phoned a precinct sergeant who I knew was disposed to do me small favors. He took Nero's number and said it might take a while at that time of day, and he would call me back. As I hung up, Fritz entered to announce dinner.

The squabs with that sauce were absolutely edible, as they always are, but other phenomena in the next couple of hours were not so pleasing. The table talk in the dining room was mostly one-sided and mostly about dogs. Wolfe kept it on a high level—no maudlin sentiment. He maintained that the basenji was the oldest breed on earth, having originated in Central Africa around 5000 B.C., whereas there was no trace of the Afghan hound earlier than around 4000 B.C. To me all it proved was that he had read a book I hadn't noticed him with.

Nero ate in the kitchen with Fritz and made a hit. Wolfe had told Fritz to call him Jet. When Fritz brought in the salad he announced that Jet had wonderful manners and was very smart.

"Nevertheless," Wolfe asked, "wouldn't you think him an insufferable nuisance as a cohabitant?"

On the contrary, Fritz declared, he would be most welcome.

After dinner, feeling that the newly formed Canine Canonizing League needed slowing down, I first took Nero out for a brief tour and, returning, escorted him up the two flights to my room and left him there. I had to admit he was well behaved. If I had wanted to take on a dog in town it could have been him. In my room I told him to lie down, and he did, and when I went to the door to leave, his eyes, which were the color of caramel, made it plain that he would love to come along, but he didn't get up.

Down in the office Wolfe and I got at the lists. They were special offerings from orchid growers and collectors from all over the world, and it was quite a job to check the thousands of items and pick the few that Wolfe might want to give a try. I sat at his desk, across from him, with trays of cards from our files, and we were in the middle of it, around ten-thirty, when the doorbell rang. I went to the hall and flipped a light switch and saw out on the stoop, through the one-way glass panel in the door, a familiar figure—Inspector Cramer of Homicide.

I went to the door, opened it six inches, and asked politely, "Now what?"

"I want to see Wolfe."

"It's pretty late. What about?"

"About a dog."

It is understood that no visitor, and especially no officer of the law, is to be conducted to the office until Wolfe has been consulted, but this seemed to rate an exception. Wolfe had been known to refuse an audience to people who topped inspectors, and, told that Cramer had come to see him about a dog, there was no telling how he might react in the situation as it had developed.

I considered the matter for about two seconds and then swung the door open and invited cordially, "Step right in."

II

"Properly speaking," Cramer declared as one who wanted above all to be perfectly fair and square, "it's Goodwin I want information from."

He was in the red leather chair at the end of Wolfe's desk, just about filling it. His big round face was no redder than usual, his gray eyes no colder, his voice no gruffer. Merely normal.

Wolfe came at me. "Then why did you bring him in here without even asking?"

Cramer interfered for me. "I asked for you. Of course you're in it. I want to know where the dog fits in. Where is it, Goodwin?"

That set the tone—again normal. He does sometimes call me Archie, after all the years, but it's exceptional. I inquired, "Dog?"

His lips tightened. "All right, I'll spell it. You phoned the precinct and gave them a tag number and wanted to know who owns the dog. When the sergeant learned that the owner was a man named Philip Kampf, who was murdered this afternoon in a house at twenty-nine Arbor Street, he notified Homicide. The officer who had been on post in front of that house had told us that the dog had gone off with a man who had said it wasn't his dog. After we learned of your inquiry about the owner, the officer was shown a picture of you and said it was you who enticed the dog. He's outside in my car. Do you want to bring him in?"

"No, thanks. I didn't entice."

"The dog followed you."

I gestured modestly. "Girls follow me, dogs follow me, sometimes even your own dicks follow me. I can't help—"

"Skip the comedy. The dog belonged to a murder victim, and you removed it from the scene of the murder. Where is it?"

Wolfe butted in. "You persist," he objected, "in imputing an action to Mr. Goodwin without warrant. He did not 'remove' the dog. I advise you to shift your ground if you expect us to listen."

His tone was firm but not hostile. I cocked an eye at

him. He was probably being indulgent because he had learned that Jet's owner was dead.

"I've got another ground," Cramer asserted. "A man who lives in that house, named Richard Meegan, and who was in it at the time Kampf was murdered, has stated that he came here to see you this morning and asked you to do a job for him. He says you refused the job. That's what he says." Cramer jutted his chin. "Now. A man at the scene of a murder admits he consulted you this morning. Goodwin shows up at the scene half an hour after the murder was committed, and he entices—okay, put it that the dog goes away with him, the dog that belonged to the victim and had gone to that house with him. How does that look?" He pulled his chin in. "You know damn well the last thing I want in a homicide is to find you or Goodwin anywhere within ten miles of it, because I know from experience what to expect. But when you're there, there you are, and I want to know how and why and what, and by God I intend to. Where's the dog?"

Wolfe sighed and shook his head. "In this instance," he said, almost genial, "you're wasting your time. As for Mr. Meegan, he phoned this morning to make an appointment and came at eleven. Our conversation was brief. He wanted a man shadowed, but divulged no name or any other specific detail because in his first breath he mentioned his wife—he was overwrought—and I gathered that his difficulty was marital. As you know, I don't touch that kind of work, and I stopped him. My vanity bristles even at an offer of that sort of job. My bluntness enraged him, and he dashed out. On his way he took his hat from the rack in the hall, and he took Mr. Goodwin's raincoat instead of his own. Archie. Proceed."

Cramer's eyes came to me, and I obeyed. "I didn't

find out about the switch in coats until the middle of the afternoon. His was the same color as mine, but mine's newer. When he phoned for an appointment this morning he gave me his name and address, and I wanted to phone him to tell him to bring my coat back, but he wasn't listed, and Information said she didn't have him, so I decided to go get it. I walked, wearing Meegan's coat. There was a cop and a crowd and a PD car in front of twenty-nine Arbor Street, and, as I approached, another PD car came, and Purley Stebbins got out and went in, so I decided to skip it, not wanting to go through the torture. There was a dog present, and he nuzzled me, and I patted him. I will admit, if pressed, that I should not have patted him. The cop asked me if the dog was mine, and I said no and went on, and headed for home. I was—"

"Did you call the dog or signal it?"

"No. I was at Twenty-eighth and Ninth Avenue before I knew he was tailing me. I did not entice or remove. If I did, if there's some kind of a dodge about the dog, please tell me why I phoned the precinct to get the name of his owner."

"I don't know. With Wolfe and you I never know. Where is it?"

I blurted it out before Wolfe could stop me. "Upstairs in my room."

"Bring it down here."

"Right."

I was up and going, but Wolfe called me sharply. "Archie!"

I turned. "Yes, sir."

"There's no frantic urgency." He went to Cramer. "The animal seems intelligent, but I doubt if it's up to answering questions. I don't want it capering around my office."

"Neither do I."

"Then why bring it down?"

"I'm taking it downtown. We want to try something with it."

Wolfe pursed his lips. "I doubt if that's feasible. Sit down, Archie. Mr. Goodwin has assumed an obligation and will have to honor it. The creature has no master, and so, presumably, no home. It will have to be tolerated here until Mr. Goodwin gets satisfactory assurance of its future welfare. Archie?"

If we had been alone I would have made my position clear, but with Cramer there I was stuck. "Absolutely," I agreed.

"You see," he told Cramer. "I'm afraid we can't permit the dog's removal."

"Nuts. I'm taking it."

"Indeed? What writ have you? Replevin? Warrant for arrest as a material witness?"

Cramer opened his mouth and shut it again. He put his elbows on the chair arms, interlaced his fingers, and leaned forward. "Look. You and Meegan check, either because you're both telling it straight, or because you've framed it, I don't know which, and we'll see. But I'm taking the dog. Kampf, the man who was killed, lived on Perry Street, a few blocks away from Arbor Street. He arrived at twenty-nine Arbor Street, with the dog on a leash, about five-twenty this afternoon. The janitor of the house, named Olsen, lives in the basement, and he was sitting at his front window, and he saw Kampf arrive with the dog and turn in at the entrance. About ten minutes later he saw the dog come out, with no leash, and right after the dog a man came out. The man was Victor Talento, a lawyer, the tenant of the ground-floor apartment. Talento says he left his apartment to go to an appointment, saw the dog in the hall, thought it was a stray, and chased it out, and that's all he knows. Anyhow, Olsen says Talento walked off, and the dog stayed there on the sidewalk."

Cramer unlaced his fingers and sat back. "About twenty minutes later, around ten minutes to six, Olsen heard someone yelling his name and went to the rear and up one flight to the ground-floor hall. Two men were there, a live one and a dead one. The live one was Ross Chaffee, a painter, the tenant of the top-floor studio—that's the fourth floor. The dead one was the man that had arrived with the dog. He had been strangled with the dog's leash, and the body was at the bottom of the stairs leading up. Chaffee says he found it when he came down to go to an appointment, and that's all he knows. He stayed there while Olsen went downstairs to phone. A squad car arrived at five-fifty-eight. Sergeant Stebbins arrived at six-ten. Goodwin arrived at six-ten. Excellent timing."

Wolfe merely grunted. Cramer continued, "You can have it all. The dog's leash was in the pocket of Kampf's raincoat, which was on him. The laboratory says it was used to strangle him. The routine is still in process. I'll answer questions within reason. The four tenants of the house were all there when Kampf arrived: Victor Talento, the lawyer, on the ground floor; Richard Meegan, whose job you say you wouldn't take, second floor; Jerome Aland, a night-club performer, third floor; and Ross Chaffee, the painter with the studio. Aland says he was sound asleep until we banged on his door and took him down to look at the corpse. Meegan says he heard nothing and knows nothing."

Cramer sat forward again. "Okay, what happened? Kampf went there to see one of those four men, and had his dog with him. It's possible he took the leash off in the lower hall to leave the dog there, but I doubt it. At least it's just as possible that he took the dog along to the door of one of the apartments, and the dog was wet and the tenant wouldn't let it enter, so Kampf left it outside. Another possibility is that the dog was actually present when Kampf was killed, but we'll know more about that after we see and handle the dog. The particular thing we want—we're going to take the dog in that house and see which door it goes to. We're going to do that now. There's a man out in my car who knows dogs." Cramer stood up.

Wolfe shook his head. "You must be hard put. You say Mr. Kampf lived on Perry Street. With a family?"

"No. Bachelor. Some kind of a writer. He didn't have to make a living; he had means."

"Then the beast is orphaned. He's in your room, Archie?"

"Yes, sir." I got up and started for the door.

Wolfe halted me. "One moment. Go up and in, lock your door, and stay there till I notify you. Go!"

I went. It was either that or quit my job on the spot, and I resign only when we haven't got company. Also, assuming that there was a valid reason for refusing to surrender the dog to the cops, Wolfe was justified. Cramer, needing no warrant to enter the house because he was already in, wouldn't hesitate to mount to my room to do his own fetching, and stopping him physically would have raised some delicate points. Whereas breaking through a locked door would be another matter.

I didn't lock it, because it hadn't been locked for years and I didn't remember which drawer of my chest the key was in, and while I was searching Cramer might conceivably have made it up the carpeted stairs and come right in, so I left it open and stood on the sill to listen. If I heard him coming I would shut it and brace it with my foot. Nero, or Jet, depending on where you stand, came over to me, but I ordered him back, and he went without a murmur. From below came voices, not cordial, but not raised enough for me to get words. Before long there was the sound of Cramer's heavy steps leaving the office and tramping along the hall, and then the slam of the front door.

I called down, "All clear?"

"No!" It was a bellow. "Wait till I bolt it!" And after a moment: "All right!"

I shut my door and went to the stairs and descended. Wolfe was back in his chair behind his desk, sitting straight. As I entered he snapped at me, "A pretty mess! You sneak a dog in here to badger me, and what now?"

I crossed to my desk, sat, and spoke calmly. "We're way beyond that. You will never admit you bollixed it up yourself, so forget it. When you ask me what now, that's easy. I could say I'll take the dog down and deliver him at Homicide, but we're beyond that too. Not only have you learned that he is orphaned, as you put it, which sounds terrible, and therefore adopting him will probably be simple, but also you have taken a stand with Cramer, and of course you won't back up. If we sit tight with the door bolted I suppose I can take the dog out back for his outings, but what if the law shows up tomorrow with a writ?"

He leaned back and shut his eyes. I looked up at the wall clock: two minutes past eleven. I looked at my wristwatch: also two minutes past eleven. They both said six minutes past when Wolfe opened his eyes.

"From Mr. Cramer's information," he said, "I doubt if that case holds any formidable difficulties."

I had no comment.

"If it were speedily solved," he went on, "your commitment to the dog could be honored at leisure. I had thought until now that my disinclination to permit a policeman to storm in here and commandeer any person or object in this house that struck his fancy was shared by you."

"It is. Within reason."

"That's an ambiguous phrase, and I must be allowed my own interpretation short of absurdity. Clearly the simplest way to settle this matter is to find out who killed Mr. Kampf. It may not be much of a job; if it proves otherwise we can reconsider. An immediate exploration is the thing, and luckily we have a pretext for it. You can go there to get your raincoat, taking Mr. Meegan's with you, and proceed as the occasion offers. The best course would be to bring him here, but, as you know, I wholly rely on your discretion and enterprise in such a juncture."

"Thank you very much," I said bitterly. "You mean now."

"Yes."

"They may still have Meegan downtown."

"I doubt if they'll keep him overnight. In the morning they'll probably have him again."

"I'll have to take the dog out first."

"Fritz will take him out back in the court."

"I'll be damned." I arose. "No client, no fee, no nothing except a dog with a wide skull for brain room." I crossed to the door, turned, said distinctly, "I will be damned," went to the rack for my hat and Meegan's coat, and beat it.

III

The rain had ended, and the wind was down. After dismissing the taxi at the end of Arbor Street, I walked to number 29, with the raincoat hung over my arm. There was light behind the curtains of the windows on the ground floor, but none anywhere above, and none in the basement. Entering the vestibule, I inspected the labels in the slots between the mailboxes and the buttons. From the bottom up they read: Talento, Meegan, Aland, and Chaffee. I pushed the button above Meegan, put my hand on the doorknob, and waited. No click. I twisted the knob, and it wouldn't turn. Another long push on the button, and a longer wait. I varied it by trying four short pushes. Nothing doing.

I left the vestibule and was confronted by two couples standing on the sidewalk staring at me, or at the entrance. They exchanged words, decided they didn't care for my returning stare, and passed on. I considered pushing the button of Victor Talento, the lawyer who lived on the ground floor, where light was showing, voted to wait a while for Meegan, with whom I had an in, moved down ten paces to a fire hydrant, and propped myself against it.

I hadn't been there long enough to shift position more than a couple of times when the light disappeared on the ground floor of number 29, and a little later the vestibule door opened and a man came out. He turned toward me, gave me a glance as he passed, and kept going. Thinking it unlikely that any occupant of that house was being extended the freedom of the city that night, I cast my eyes around, and sure enough, when the subject had gone some thirty paces a figure emerged from an areaway across the street and started strolling. I shook my head in disapproval. I would have waited until the guy was ten paces farther. Saul Panzer would have made it ten more than that, but Saul is the best tailer alive.

As I stood deploring that faulty performance, an idea hit me. They might keep Meegan downtown another two hours, or all night, or he might even be up in his bed asleep. This was at least a chance to take a stab at something. I shoved off, in the direction taken by the subject, who was now a block away. Stepping along, I gained on him. A little beyond the corner I was abreast of the city employee, who was keeping to the other side of the street; but I wasn't interested in him. It seemed to me that the subject was upping the stroke a little, so I did too, really marching, and as he reached the next intersection I was beside him. He had looked over his shoulder when he heard me coming up behind, but hadn't slowed. As I reached him I spoke.

"Victor Talento?"

"No comment," he said and kept going. So did I.

"Thanks for the compliment," I said, "but I'm not a reporter. My name's Archie Goodwin, and I work for Nero Wolfe. If you'll stop a second I'll show you my credentials."

"I'm not interested in your credentials."

"Okay. If you just came out for a breath of air you won't be interested in this either. Otherwise you may be. Please don't scream or look around, but you've got a Homicide dick on your tail. Don't look or he'll know I'm telling you. He's across the street, ninety feet back."

"Yes," he conceded, without changing pace, "that's interesting. Is this your good deed for the day?"

"No. I'm out dowsing for Mr. Wolfe. He's investigating a murder just for practice, and I'm looking for a seam. I thought if I gave you a break you might feel like reciprocating. If you're just out for a walk, forget it, and sorry I interrupted. If you're headed for something you'd like to keep private maybe you could use some expert advice. In this part of town at this time of night there are only two approved methods for shaking a tail, and I'd be glad to oblige."

He looked it over for half a block, with me keeping step, and then spoke. "You mentioned credentials."

"Right. We might as well stop under that light. The dick will keep his distance."

We stopped. I got out my wallet and let him have a look at my licenses, detective and driver's. He didn't skimp it, being a lawyer. I put my wallet back.

"Of course," he said, "I was aware that I might be followed."

"Sure."

"I intended to take precautions. But it may not be —I suppose it's not as simple as it seems. I have had no experience at this kind of maneuver. Who hired Wolfe to investigate?"

"I don't know. He says he needs practice."

"All right, if it's qualified." He stood sizing me up by the street light. He was an inch shorter than me, and some older, with his weight starting to collect around the middle. He was dark-skinned, with eyes to match, and his nose hooked to point down. I didn't prod him. My lucky stab had snagged him, and it was his problem. He was working on it.

"I have an appointment," he said.

I waited.

He went on. "A woman phoned me, and I arranged to meet her. My wire could have been tapped."

"I doubt it. They're not that fast."

"I suppose not. The woman had nothing to do with

the murder, and neither had I, but of course anything I do and anyone I see is suspect. I have no right to expose her to possible embarrassment, and I can't be sure of shaking that man off."

I grinned at him. "And me too."

"You mean you would follow me?"

"Certainly, for practice. And I'd like to see how you handle it."

He wasn't returning my grin. "I see you've earned your reputation, Goodwin. You'd be wasting your time, because this woman has no connection with this business, but I should have known better than to make this appointment. I won't keep it. It's only three blocks from here. You might be willing to go and tell her I'm not coming, and I'll get in touch with her tomorrow. Yes?"

"Sure, if it's only three blocks. If you'll return the favor by calling on Nero Wolfe for a little talk. That's what I meant by reciprocating."

He considered it. "Not tonight."

"Tonight would be best."

"No. I'm all in."

"Tomorrow morning at eleven?"

"Yes, I can make it then."

"Okay." I gave him the address. "If you forget it, it's in the book. Now brief me."

He took a respectable roll of bills from his pocket and peeled off a twenty. "Since you're acting as my agent, you have a right to a fee."

I grinned again. "That's a neat idea, you being a lawyer, but I'm not acting as your agent. I'm doing you a favor on request and expecting one in return. Where's the appointment?"

He put the roll back. "Have it your way. The woman's name is Jewel Jones, and she's at the south-east corner of Christopher and Grove Streets, or will be." He looked at his wrist. "We were to meet there at midnight. She's medium height, slender, dark hair and eyes, very goodlooking. Tell her why I'm not coming, and say she'll hear from me tomorrow."

"Right. You'd better take a walk in the other direction to keep the dick occupied, and don't look back."

He wanted to shake hands to show his appreciation, but that would have been just as bad as taking the twenty, since before another midnight Wolfe might be tagging him for murder, so I pretended not to notice. He headed east, and I headed west, moving right along without turning my head for a glimpse of the dick. I had to make sure that he didn't see a vision and switch subjects, but I let that wait until I got to Christopher Street. Reaching it, I turned the corner, went twenty feet to a stoop, slid behind it with only my head out, and counted a slow hundred. There were passers-by, a couple and a guy in a hurry, but no dick. I went on a block to Grove Street, passed the intersection, saw no loitering female, continued for a distance, and turned and backtracked. I was on the fifth lap, and it was eight minutes past twelve, when a taxi stopped at the corner, a woman got out, and the taxi rolled off.

I approached. The light could have been better, but she seemed to meet the specifications. I stopped and asked, "Jones?" She drew herself up. I said, "From Victor."

She tilted her head back to get my face. "Who are you?" She seemed a little out of breath.

"Victor sent me with a message, but naturally I have to be sure it reaches the right party. I've ante'd half of your name and half of his, so it's your turn."

"Who are you?"

I shook my head. "You go first, or no message from Victor."

"Where is he?"

"No. I'll count ten and go. One, two, three, four—"

"My name is Jewel Jones. His is Victor Talento."

"That's the girl. I'll tell you." I did so. Since it was desirable for her to grasp the situation fully, I started with my propping myself on the fire hydrant in front of 29 Arbor Street and went on from there, as it happened, including, of course, my name and status. By the time I finished she had developed a healthy frown.

"Damn it," she said with feeling. She moved and put a hand on my arm. "Come and put me in a taxi."

I stayed planted. "I'll be glad to, and it will be on me. We're going to Nero Wolfe's place."

"We?" She removed the hand. "You're crazy."

"One will get you ten I'm not. Look at it. You and Talento made an appointment at a street corner, so you had some good reason for not wanting to be seen together tonight. It must have been something fairly urgent. I admit the urgency didn't have to be connected with the murder of Philip Kampf, but it could be, and it certainly has to be discussed. I don't want to be arbitrary. I can take you to a Homicide sergeant named Stebbins, and you can discuss it with him; or I'll take you to Mr. Wolfe. I should think you'd prefer Mr. Wolfe, but suit yourself."

She had well-oiled gears. For a second, as I spoke, her eyes flashed like daggers, but then they went soft and appealing. She took my arm again, this time with both hands. "I'll discuss it with you," she said, in a voice she could have used to defrost her refrigerator. "I wouldn't mind that. We'll go somewhere."

I said come on, and we moved, with her maintaining contact with a hand hooked cozily on my arm. We hadn't gone far, toward Seventh Avenue, when a taxi came along and I flagged it and we got in. I told the driver, "Nine-eighteen West Thirty-fifth," and he started.

"What's that?" Miss Jones demanded.

I told her, Nero Wolfe's house. The poor girl didn't know what to do. If she called me a rat that wouldn't help her any. If she kicked and screamed I would merely give the hackie another address. Her best bet was to try to thaw me, and if she had had time for a real campaign, say four or five hours, she might conceivably have made some progress, because she had a knack for it. She didn't coax or argue; she just told me how she knew I was the kind of man she could tell anything to and I would believe her and understand her, and after she had done that she would be willing to go anywhere or do anything I advised, but she was sure I wouldn't want to take advantage . . .

There just wasn't time enough. The taxi rolled to the curb, and I had a bill ready for the driver. I got out, gave her a hand, and escorted her up the seven steps of the stoop, applauding her economy in not wasting breath on protests. My key wouldn't let us in, since the chain bolt would be on, so I pushed the button, and in a moment the stoop light shone on us, and in another the door opened. I motioned her in and followed. Fritz was there.

"Mr. Wolfe up?" I asked.

"In the office." He was giving Miss Jones a look, the look he gives any strange female who enters that house. There is always in his mind the possibility, however remote, that she will bewitch Wolfe into a mania for a mate. After asking him to conduct her to the front room, and putting my hat and the raincoat on the rack, I went on down the hall and entered the office.

Wolfe was at his desk, reading, and curled up in the middle of the room, on the best rug in the house, which was given to Wolfe years ago as a token of gratitude by an Armenian merchant who had got himself in a bad hole, was the dog. The dog greeted me by lifting his head and tapping the rug with his tail. Wolfe greeted me by raising his eyes from the book and grunting.

"I brought company," I told him. "Before I introduce her I should—"

"Her? The tenants of that house are all men! I might have known you'd dig up a woman!"

"I can chase her if you don't want her. This is how I got her." I proceeded, not dragging it out, but including all the essentials. I ended up, "I could have taken her to a spot I know of and grilled her myself, but it would have been risky. Just in a six-minute taxi ride she had me feeling—uh, brotherly. Do you want her or not?"

"Confound it." His eyes went to his book and stayed there long enough to finish a paragraph. He dog-eared it and put it down. "Very well, bring her."

I crossed to the connecting door to the front room, opened it, and requested, "Please come in, Miss Jones." She came, and as she passed through gave me a wistful smile that might have gone straight to my heart if there hadn't been a diversion. As she entered, the dog suddenly sprang to his feet, whirling, and made for her with sounds of unmistakable pleasure. He stopped in front of her, raising his head so she wouldn't have to reach far to pat it, and wagged his tail so fast it was only a blur.

"Indeed," Wolfe said. "How do you do, Miss Jones. I am Nero Wolfe. What's the dog's name?"

I claim she was good. The presence of the dog was a complete surprise to her. But without the slightest sign of fluster she put out a hand to give it a gentle pat, looked around, spotted the red leather chair, went to it, and sat.

"That's a funny question right off," she said, not complaining. "Asking me your dog's name."

"Pfui." Wolfe was disgusted. "I don't know what position you were going to take, but from what Mr. Goodwin tells me I would guess you were going to say that the purpose of your appointment with Mr. Talento was a personal matter that had nothing to do with Mr. Kampf or his death, and that you knew Mr. Kampf either slightly and casually or not at all. Now the dog has made that untenable. Obviously he knows you well, and he belonged to Mr. Kampf. So you knew Mr. Kampf well. If you try to deny that you'll have Mr. Goodwin and other trained men digging all around you, your past and your present, and that will be extremely disagreeable, no matter how innocent you may be of murder or any other wrongdoing. You won't like that. What's the dog's name?"

She looked at me, and I met it. In good light I would have qualified Talento's specification of "very good-looking." Not that she was unsightly, but she caught the eye more by what she looked than how she looked. It wasn't just something she turned on as needed; it was there even now, when she must have been pretty busy deciding how to handle it.

It took her only a few seconds to decide. "His name is Bootsy," she said. The dog, at her feet, lifted his head and wagged his tail.

"Good heavens," Wolfe muttered. "No other name?"

"Not that I know of."

"Your name is Jewel Jones?"

"Yes. I sing in a night club, the Flamingo, but I'm

not working right now." She made a little gesture, very appealing, but it was Wolfe who had to resist it, not me. "Believe me, Mr. Wolfe, I don't know anything about that murder. If I knew anything that could help I'd be perfectly willing to tell you, because I'm sure you're the kind of man that understands and you wouldn't want to hurt me if you didn't have to."

That wasn't what she had fed me verbatim. Not verbatim.

"I try to understand," Wolfe said dryly. "You knew Mr. Kampf intimately?"

"Yes, I guess so." She smiled as one understander to another. "For a while I did. Not lately, not for the past two months."

"You met the dog at his apartment on Perry Street?"

"That's right. For nearly a year I was there quite often."

"You and Mr. Kampf quarreled?"

"Oh no, we didn't quarrel. I just didn't see him any more. I had other—I was very busy."

"When did you see him last?"

"Well—you mean intimately?"

"No. At all."

"About two weeks ago, at the club. He came to the club once or twice and spoke to me there."

"But no quarrel?"

"No, there was nothing to quarrel about."

"You have no idea who killed him, or why?"

"I certainly haven't."

Wolfe leaned back. "Do you know Mr. Talento intimately?"

"No, not if you mean—of course we're friends. I used to live there."

"With Mr. Talento?"

"Not *with* him." She was mildly shocked. "I never live with a man. I had the second-floor apartment."

"At twenty-nine Arbor Street?"

"Yes."

"For how long? When?"

"For nearly a year. I left there—let's see—about three months ago. I have a little apartment on East Forty-ninth Street."

"Then you know the others too? Mr. Meegan and Mr. Chaffee and Mr. Aland?"

"I know Ross Chaffee and Jerry Aland, but no Meegan. Who's he?"

"A tenant at twenty-nine Arbor Street. Second floor."

She nodded. "Well, sure, that's the floor I had." She smiled. "I hope they fixed that damn table for him. That was one reason I left. I hate furnished apartments, don't you?"

Wolfe made a face. "In principle, yes. I take it you now have your own furniture. Supplied by Mr. Kampf?"

She laughed—more of a chuckle—and her eyes danced. "I see you didn't know Phil Kampf."

"Not supplied by him, then?"

"A great big no."

"By Mr. Chaffee? Or Mr. Aland?"

"No and no." She went very earnest. "Look, Mr. Wolfe. A friend of mine was mighty nice about that furniture, and we'll just leave it. Archie told me what you're interested in is the murder, and I'm sure you wouldn't want to drag in a lot of stuff just to hurt me and a friend of mine, so we'll forget the furniture."

Wolfe didn't press it. He took a hop. "Your appointment on a street corner with Mr. Talento—what was that about?"

She nodded. "I've been wondering about that. I mean what I would say when you asked me, because I'd hate to have you think I'm a sap, and I guess it sounds like it. I phoned him when I heard on the radio about Phil and where he was killed, there on Arbor Street, and I knew Vic still lived there and I simply wanted to ask him about it."

"You had him on the phone."

"He didn't seem to want to talk about it on the phone."

"But why a street corner?"

This time it was more like a laugh. "Now, Mr. Wolfe, you're not a sap. You asked about the furniture, didn't you? Well, a girl with furniture shouldn't be seen places with a man like Vic Talento."

"What is he like?"

She fluttered a hand. "Oh, he wants to get close."

Wolfe kept at her until after one o'clock, and I could report it all, but it wouldn't get you any further than it did him. He couldn't trip her or back her into a corner. She hadn't been to Arbor Street for two months. She hadn't seen Chaffee or Aland or Talento for weeks, and of course not Meegan, since she had never heard of him before. She couldn't even try to guess who had killed Kampf. The only thing remotely to be regarded as a return on Wolfe's investment of a full hour was her statement that as far as she knew there was no one who had both an attachment and a claim to Bootsy. If there were heirs she had no idea who they were. When she left the chair to go the dog got up too, and she patted him, and he went with us to the door. I took her to Tenth Avenue and put her in a taxi, and returned.

I got a glass of milk from the kitchen and took it to the office. Wolfe, who was drinking beer, didn't scowl at me. He seldom scowls when he is drinking beer.

"Where's Bootsy?" I inquired.

"No," he said emphatically.

"Okay." I surrendered. "Where's Jet?"

"Down in Fritz's room. He'll sleep there. You don't like him."

"That's not true, but you can have it. It means you can't blame him on me, and that suits me fine." I sipped milk. "Anyhow, that will no longer be an issue after Homicide comes in the morning with a document and takes him away."

"They won't come."

"I offer twenty to one. Before noon."

He nodded. "That was roughly my own estimate of the probability, so while you were out I phoned Mr. Cramer. I suggested an arrangement, and I suppose he inferred that if he declined the arrangement the dog might be beyond his jurisdiction before tomorrow, though I didn't say so. I may have given that impression."

"Yeah. You should be more careful."

"So the arrangement has been made. You are to be at twenty-nine Arbor Street, with the dog, at nine o'clock in the morning. You are to be present throughout the fatuous performance the police have in mind, and keep the dog in view. The dog is to leave the premises with you, before noon, and you are to bring him back here. The police are to make no further effort to constrain the dog for twenty-four hours. While in that house you may find an opportunity to flush something or someone more contributive than that volatile demi-rep. If you will come to my room before you go in the morning I may have a suggestion."

"I resent that," I said manfully. "When you call her that, smile."

IV

It was a fine bright morning. I didn't take Meegan's raincoat, because I didn't need any pretext and I doubted if the program would offer a likely occasion for the exchange.

The law was there in front, waiting for me. The one who knew dogs was a stocky middle-aged guy who wore rimless glasses. Before he touched the dog he asked me the name, and I told him Bootsy.

"A hell of a name," he observed. "Also that's a hell of a leash you've got."

"I agree. His was on the corpse, so I suppose it's in the lab." I handed him my end of the heavy cord. "If he bites you it's not on me."

"He won't bite me. Would you, Bootsy?" He squatted before the dog and started to get acquainted. Sergeant Purley Stebbins growled, a foot from my ear, "He should have bit you when you kidnapped him."

I turned. Purley was half an inch taller than me and two inches broader. "You've got it twisted," I told him. "It's women that bite me. I've often wondered what would bite you."

We continued exchanging pleasantries while the dog man, whose name was Loftus, made friends with Bootsy. It wasn't long before he announced that he was ready to proceed. He was frowning. "In a way," he said, "it would be better to keep him on leash after I go in, because Kampf probably did. Or did he? Maybe you ought to brief me a little more. How much do we know?"

"To swear to," Purley told him, "damn little. But putting it all together from what we've collected, this is how it looks, and I'll have to be shown different. When Kampf and the dog entered it was raining and the dog was wet. Kampf left the dog in the ground-floor hall. He removed the leash and had it in his hand when he went to the door of one of the apartments. The tenant of the apartment let him in, and they talked. The tenant socked him, probably from behind without warning, and used the leash to finish him. He stuffed the leash in the pocket of the raincoat. It took nerve and muscle both to carry the body out and down the stairs to the lower hall, but he damn well had to get it out of his place and away from his door, and any of those four could have done it in a pinch, and it sure was a pinch. Of course the dog was already outside, out on the sidewalk. While Kampf was in one of the apartments getting killed, Talento had come into the lower hall and seen the dog and chased it out."

"Then," Loftus objected, "Talento's clean."

"No. Nobody's clean. If it was Talento, after he killed Kampf he went out to the hall and put the dog out in the vestibule, went back in his apartment and carried the body out and dumped it at the foot of the stairs, and then left the house, chasing the dog on out to the sidewalk. You're the dog expert. Is there anything wrong with that?"

"Not necessarily. It depends on the dog and how close he was to Kampf. There wasn't any blood."

"Then that's how I'm buying it. If you want it filled in you can spend the rest of the day with the reports of the other experts and the statements of the tenants."

"Some other day. That'll do for now. You're going in first?"

"Yeah. Come on, Goodwin."

Purley started for the door, but I objected. "I'm staying with the dog."

"For God's sake. Then keep behind Loftus."

I changed my mind. It would be interesting to

watch the experiment, and from behind Loftus the view wouldn't be good. So I went into the vestibule with Purley. The inner door was opened by a Homicide colleague, and we crossed the threshold and moved to the far side of the small lobby, which was fairly clean but not ornate. The colleague closed the door and stayed there. In a minute he pulled it open again, and Loftus and the dog entered. Two steps in, Loftus stopped, and so did the dog. No one spoke. The leash hung limp. Bootsy looked around at Loftus. Loftus bent over and untied the cord from the collar, and held it up to show Bootsy he was free. Bootsy came over to me and stood, his head up, wagging his tail.

"Nuts," Purley said, disgusted.

"You know what I really expected," Loftus said. "I never thought he'd show us where Kampf took him when they entered yesterday, but I did think he'd go to the foot of the stairs, where the body was found, and I thought he might go on to where the body came from —Talento's door, or upstairs. Take him by the collar, Goodwin, and ease him over to the foot of the stairs."

I obliged. He came without urging, but gave no sign that the spot held any special interest for him. We all stood and watched him. He opened his mouth wide to yawn.

"Fine," Purley rumbled. "Just fine. You might as well go on with it."

Loftus came and fastened the leash to the collar, led Bootsy across the lobby to a door, and knocked. In a moment the door opened, and there was Victor Talento in a fancy rainbow dressing gown.

"Hello, Bootsy," he said, and reached down to pat.

"Goddamit!" Purley barked. "I told you not to speak!"

Talento straightened up. "So you did." He was apologetic. "I'm sorry, I forgot. Do you want to try it again?"

"No. That's all."

Talento backed in and closed the door.

"You must realize," Loftus told Purley, "that a Labrador can't be expected to go for a man's throat. They're not that kind of dog. The most you could expect would be an attitude, or possibly a growl."

"You can have 'em," Purley growled. "Is it worth going on?"

"By all means. You'd better go first."

Purley headed for me, and I gave him room and then followed him up the stairs. The upper hall was narrow and not very light, with a door at the rear end and another toward the front. We backed up against the wall opposite the front door to leave enough space for Loftus and Bootsy. They came, Bootsy tagging, and Loftus knocked. Ten seconds passed before footsteps sounded, and then the door was opened by the specimen who had dashed out of Wolfe's place the day before and taken my coat with him. He was in his shirt sleeves, and he hadn't combed his hair.

"This is Sergeant Loftus, Mr. Meegan," Purley said. "Take a look at the dog. Have you ever seen it before? Pat it."

Meegan snorted. "Pat it yourself. Go to hell."

"Have you ever seen it before?"

"No."

"Okay, thanks. Come on, Loftus."

As we started up the next flight the door slammed behind us, good and loud. Purley asked over his shoulder, "Well?"

"He didn't like him," Loftus replied from the rear, "but there are lots of people lots of dogs don't like."

The third-floor hall was a duplicate of the one below. Again Purley and I posted ourselves opposite the door, and Loftus came with Bootsy and knocked. Nothing happened. He knocked again, louder, and pretty soon the door opened to a two-inch crack, and a squeaky voice came through.

"You've got the dog."

"Right here," Loftus told him.

"Are you there, Sergeant?"

"Right here," Purley answered.

"I told you that dog don't like me. Once at a party at Phil Kampf's—I told you. I didn't mean to hurt it, but it thought I did. What are you trying to do, frame me?"

"Open the door. The dog's on a leash."

"I won't! I told you I wouldn't!"

Purley moved. His arm, out stiff, went over Loftus's shoulder, and his palm met the door and kept going. The door hesitated an instant and then swung open. Standing there, holding to its edge, was a skinny individual in red-and-green-striped pajamas. The dog let out a low growl and backed up a little.

"We're making the rounds, Mr. Aland," Purley said, "and we couldn't leave you out. Now you can go back to sleep. As for trying to frame you—"

He stopped because the door shut.

"You didn't tell me," Loftus complained, "that Aland had already fixed it for a reaction."

"No, I thought I'd wait and see. One to go." He headed for the stairs.

The top-floor hall had had someone's personal attention. It was no bigger than the others, but it had a nice clean tan-colored runner, and the walls were painted the same shade and sported a few small pictures. Purley went to the rear door instead of the front, and we made room for Loftus and Bootsy by flattening against the wall. When Loftus knocked footsteps responded at once, approaching the door, and it swung wide open. This was the painter, Ross Chaffee, and he was dressed for it, in an old brown smock. He was by far the handsomest of the tenants, tall, erect, with artistic wavy dark hair and features he must have enjoyed looking at.

I had ample time to enjoy them too as he stood smiling at us, completely at ease, obeying Purley's prior instructions not to speak. Bootsy was also at ease. When it became quite clear that no blood was going to be shed, Purley asked, "You know the dog, don't you, Mr. Chaffee?"

"Certainly. He's a beautiful animal."

"Pat him."

"With pleasure." He bent gracefully. "Bootsy, do you know your master's gone?" He scratched behind the black ears. "Gone forever, Bootsy, and that's too bad." He straightened. "Anything else? I'm working. I like the morning light."

"That's all, thanks." Purley turned to go, and I let Loftus and Bootsy by before following. On the way down the three flights no one had any remarks.

As we hit the level of the lower hall Victor Talento's door opened, and he emerged and spoke. "The District Attorney's office phoned. Are you through with me? They want me down there."

"We're through," Purley rumbled. "We can run you down."

Talento said that would be fine and he would be ready in a minute. Purley told Loftus to give me Bootsy, and he handed me the leash.

"I am willing," I said helpfully, "to give you a detailed analysis of the dog's conduct. It will take about a week."

"Go to hell," Purley growled, "and take the goddam dog along."

I departed. Outside the morning was still fine. The presence of two PD cars in front of the scene of a murder had attracted a small gathering, and Bootsy and I were objects of interest as we appeared and started off. We both ignored the stares. We moseyed along, in no hurry, stopping now and then to give Bootsy a chance to inspect something if he felt inclined. At the fourth or fifth stop, more than a block away, I saw the quartet leaving number 29. Stebbins and Talento took one car and Loftus and the colleague the other, and they rolled off.

I shortened up on Bootsy a little, walked him west until an empty taxi appeared, stopped it and got in, took a five-dollar bill from my wallet, and handed it to the hackie.

"Thanks," he said with feeling. "For what, down payment on the cab?"

"You'll earn it, brother," I assured him. "Is there somewhere within a block or so of Arbor and Court where you can park for anywhere from thirty minutes to three hours?"

"Not three hours for a finif."

"Of course not." I got another five and gave it to him. "I doubt if it will be that long."

"There's a parking lot not too far. On the street without a passenger I'll be solicited."

"You'll have a passenger—the dog. I prefer the street. He's a nice dog. When I return I'll be reasonable. Let's see what we can find."

He pulled the lever and we moved. There are darned few legal parking spaces in all Manhattan at that time of day, and we cruised around several corners before we found one, on Court Street two blocks from Arbor. He backed into it and I got out, leaving the windows down three inches. I told him I'd be back when he saw me, and headed south, turning right at the second corner.

There was no police car at 29 Arbor, and no gathering. That was satisfactory. Entering the vestibule, I pushed the button under Meegan and put my hand on the knob. No click. Pushing twice more and still getting no response, I tried Aland's button, and that worked. After a short wait the click came, and I shoved the door open, entered, mounted two flights, went to the door, and knocked with authority.

The squeaky voice came through. "Who is it?"

"Goodwin. I was just here with the others. I haven't got the dog. Open up."

The door swung slowly to a crack, and then wider. Jerome Aland was still in his gaudy pajamas. "For God's sake," he squeaked, "what do you want now? I need some sleep!"

I didn't apologize. "I was going to ask you some questions when I was here before," I told him, "but the dog complicated it. It won't take long." Since he wasn't polite enough to move aside, I had to brush him, skinny as he was, as I went in. "Which way?"

He slid past me, and I followed him across to chairs. They were the kind of chairs that made Jewel Jones hate furnished apartments, and the rest of the furniture didn't help any. He sat on the edge of one and demanded, "All right, what?"

It was a little tricky. Since he was assuming I was one of the Homicide personnel, it wouldn't do for me to know either too much or too little. It would be risky to mention Jewel Jones, because the cops might not have got around to her at all.

"I'm checking some points," I told him. "How long

has Richard Meegan occupied the apartment below
you?"

"Hell, I've told you that a dozen times."

"Not me. I said I'm checking. How long?"

"Nine days. He took it a week ago Tuesday."

"Who was the previous tenant? Just before him."

"There wasn't any. It was empty."

"Empty ever since you've been here?"

"No, I've told you, a girl had it, but she moved out
about three months ago. Her name is Jewel Jones, and
she's a fine artist, and she got me my job at the night
club where I work now." His mouth worked. "I know
what you're doing, you're trying to make it nasty, and
you're trying to catch me getting my facts twisted.
Bringing that dog here to growl at me—can I help it if
I don't like dogs?"

He ran his fingers, both hands, through his hair.
When the hair was messed good he gestured like a
night-club performer. "Die like a dog," he said. "That's
what Phil did, died like a dog. Poor Phil, I wouldn't
want to see that again."

"You said," I ventured, "that you and he were good
friends."

His head jerked up. "I did not. Did I say that?"

"More or less. Maybe not in those words. Why,
weren't you?"

"We were not. I haven't got any good friends."

"You just said that the girl that used to live here
got you a job. That sounds like a good friend. Or did
she owe you something?"

"Not a damn thing. Why do you keep bringing her
up?"

"I didn't bring her up, you did. I only asked who
was the former tenant in the apartment below you.
Why, would you rather keep her out of it?"

"I don't have to keep her out. She's not in it."

"Perhaps not. Did she know Philip Kampf?"

"I guess so. Sure she did."

"How well did she know him?"

He shook his head. "Now you're getting personal, and I'm the wrong person. If Phil was alive you could ask him, and he might tell you. Me, I don't know."

I smiled at him. "All that does, Mr. Aland, is make me curious. Somebody in this house murdered Kampf. So we ask you questions, and when we come to one you shy at, naturally we wonder why. If you don't like talking about Kampf and that girl, think what it could mean. For instance, it could mean that the girl was yours, and Kampf took her away from you, and that was why you killed him when he came here yesterday. Or it could—"

"She wasn't mine!"

"Uh-huh. Or it could mean that although she wasn't yours, you were under a deep obligation to her, and Kampf had given her a dirty deal, or he was threatening her with something, and she wanted him disposed of, and you obliged. Or of course it could be merely that Kampf had something on you."

He had his head tilted back so he could look down on me. "You're in the wrong racket," he asserted. "You ought to be writing TV scripts."

I stuck with him only a few more minutes, having got all I could hope for under the circumstances. Since I was letting him assume that I was a city employee, I couldn't very well try to pry him loose for a trip to Wolfe's place. Also I had two more calls to make, and there was no telling when I might be interrupted by a phone call or a courier to one of them from downtown. The only further item I gathered from Jerome Aland was that he wasn't trying to get from under by slipping in any insinuations about his co-tenants. He had no opinions or ideas about who had killed poor Phil. When I left he stood up, but he let me go and open the door for myself.

I went down a flight, to Meegan's door, and knocked and waited. Just as I was raising a fist to make it louder and better there were footsteps inside, and the door opened. Meegan was still in his shirt sleeves and still uncombed.

"Well?" he demanded.

"Back again," I said firmly but not offensively. "With a few questions. If you don't mind?"

"You know damn well I mind."

"Naturally. Mr. Talento has been called down to the District Attorney's office. This might possibly save you another trip there."

He sidestepped, and I went in. The room was the same size and shape as Aland's, above, and the furniture, though different, was no more desirable. The table against a wall was lopsided—probably the one that Jewel Jones hoped they had fixed for him. I took a chair at its end, and he took another and sat frowning at me.

"Haven't I seen you before?" he wanted to know.

"Sure, we were here with the dog."

"I mean before that. Wasn't it you in Nero Wolfe's office yesterday?"

"That's right."

"How come?"

I raised my brows. "Haven't you got the lines crossed, Mr. Meegan? I'm here to ask questions, not to answer them. I was in Wolfe's office on business. I often am. Now—"

"He's a fat, arrogant halfwit!"

"You may be right. He's certainly arrogant. Now,

I'm here on business." I got out my notebook and pencil. "You moved into this place nine days ago. Please tell me exactly how you came to take this apartment."

He glared. "I've told it at least three times."

"I know. This is the way it's done. I'm not trying to catch you in some little discrepancy, but you could have omitted something important. Just assume I haven't heard it before. Go ahead."

"Oh, my God." His head dropped and his lips tightened. Normally he might not have been a bad-looking guy, with blond hair and gray eyes and a long bony face, but now, having spent the night, or most of it, with Homicide and the DA, he looked it, especially his eyes, which were red and puffy.

He lifted his head. "I'm a commercial photographer —in Pittsburgh. Two years ago I married a girl named Margaret Ryan. Seven months later she left me. I didn't know whether she went alone or with somebody. She just left. She left Pittsburgh too, or anyway I couldn't find her there, and her family never saw her or heard from her. About five months later, about a year ago, a man I know, a businessman I do work for, came back from a trip to New York and said he'd seen her in a theater here with a man. He went and spoke to her, but she claimed he was mistaken. He was sure it was her. I came to New York and spent a week looking around but didn't find her. I didn't go to the police because I didn't want to. You want a better reason, but that's mine."

"I'll skip that." I was writing in the notebook. "Go ahead."

"Two weeks ago I went to look at a show of pictures at the Institute in Pittsburgh. There was a painting there, an oil, a big one. It was called 'Three Young Mares at Pasture,' and it was an interior, a room, with three women in it. One of them was on a couch, and two of them were on a rug on the floor. They were eating apples. The one on the couch was my wife. I was sure of it the minute I saw her, and after I stood and studied it I was even surer. There was absolutely no doubt of it."

"We're not challenging that," I assured him. "What did you do?"

"The artist's signature looked like Chapple, but of course the catalogue settled that. It was Ross Chaffee. I went to the Institute office and asked about him. They thought he lived in New York but weren't sure. I had some work on hand I had to finish, and it took a couple of days, and then I came to New York. I had no trouble finding Ross Chaffee; he was in the phone book. I went to see him at his studio—here in this house. First I told him I was interested in that figure in his painting, that I thought she would be just right to model for some photographs I wanted to do, but he said that his opinion of photography as a medium was such that he wouldn't care to supply models for it, and he was bowing me out, so I told him how it was. I told him the whole thing. Then he was different. He sympathized with me and said he would be glad to help me if he could, but he had painted that picture more than a year ago, and he used so many different models for his pictures that it was impossible to remember which was which."

Meegan stopped, and I looked up from the note-book. He said aggressively, "I'm repeating that that sounded phony to me."

"Go right ahead. You're telling it."

"I say it was phony. A photographer might use hundreds of models in a year, and he might forget, but not a painter. Not a picture like that. I got a little tactless with him, and then I apologized. He said he might be able to refresh his memory and asked me to phone him the next day. Instead of phoning I went back the next day to see him, but he said he simply couldn't remember and doubted if he ever could. I didn't get tactless again. Coming in the house, I had noticed a sign that there was a furnished apartment to let, and when I left Chaffee I found the janitor and rented it, and went to my hotel for my bags and moved in. I knew damn well my wife had modeled for that picture, and I knew I could find her. I wanted to be as close as I could to Chaffee and the people who came to see him."

I wanted something too. I wanted to say that he must have had a photograph of his wife along and that I would like to see it, but of course I didn't dare, since it was a cinch that he had already either given it to the cops, or refused to, or claimed he didn't have one. So I merely asked, "What progress did you make?"

"Not much. I tried to get friendly with Chaffee but didn't get very far. I met the other two tenants, Talento and Aland, but that didn't get me anywhere. Finally I decided I would have to get some expert help, and that was why I went to see Nero Wolfe. You were there, you know how that came out—that big blob."

I nodded. "He has dropsy of the ego. What did you want him to do?"

"I've told you."

"Tell it again."

"I was going to have him tap Chaffee's phone."

"That's illegal," I said severely.

"All right, I didn't do it."

I flipped a page of the notebook. "Go back a little.

During that week, besides the tenants here, how many of Chaffee's friends and acquaintances did you meet?"

"Just two, as I've told you. A young woman, a model, in his studio one day, and I don't remember her name, and a man that was there another day, a man that Chaffee said buys his pictures. His name was Braunstein."

"You're leaving out Philip Kampf."

Meegan leaned forward and put a fist on the table. "Yes, and I'm going to leave him out. I never saw him or heard of him."

"What would you say if I said you were seen with him?"

"I'd say you were a dirty liar!" The red eyes looked redder. "As if I wasn't already having enough trouble, now you set on me about a murder of a man I never heard of! You bring a dog here and tell me to pat it, for God's sake!"

I nodded. "That's your hard luck, Mr. Meegan. You're not the first man that's had a murder for company without inviting it." I closed the notebook and put it in my pocket. "You'd better find some way of handling your troubles without having people's phones tapped." I arose. "Stick around, please. You may be wanted downtown anyhow."

He went to open the door for me. I would have liked to get more details of his progress with Ross Chaffee, or lack of it, and his contacts with the other two tenants, but it seemed more important to have some words with Chaffee before I got interrupted. As I mounted the two flights to the top floor my wristwatch said twenty-eight minutes past ten.

V

"I know there's no use complaining," Ross Chaffee said, "about these interruptions to my work. Under the circumstances." He was being very gracious about it.

The top floor was quite different from the others. I don't know what his living quarters in front were like, but the studio, in the rear, was big and high and anything but crummy. There were sculptures around, big and little, and canvases of all sizes were stacked and propped against racks. The walls were covered with drapes, solid gray, with nothing on them. Each of two easels—one much larger than the other—held a canvas that had been worked on. There were several plain chairs and two upholstered ones, and an oversized divan, nearly square. I had been steered to one of the upholstered numbers, and Chaffee, still in his smock, had moved a plain one to sit facing me.

"Only don't prolong it unnecessarily," he requested.

I said I wouldn't. "There are a couple of points," I told him, "that we wonder about a little. Of course it could be merely a coincidence that Richard Meegan came to town looking for his wife, and came to see you, and rented an apartment here just nine days before Kampf was murdered, but a coincidence like that will have to stand some going over. Frankly, Mr. Chaffee, there are those, and I happen to be one of them, who find it hard to believe that you couldn't remember who modeled for an important figure in a picture you painted. I know what you say, but it's still hard to believe."

"My dear sir." Chaffee was smiling. "Then you must think I'm lying."

"I didn't say so."

"But you do, of course." He shrugged. "To what
end? What deep design am I cherishing?"

"I wouldn't know. You say you wanted to help Meegan find his wife."

"No, not that I wanted to. I was willing to. He was
a horrible nuisance."

"He must have been a first-class pest."

"He was. He is."

"It should have been worth some effort to get rid of
him. Did you make any?"

"I have explained what I did—in a statement, and
signed it. I have nothing to add. I tried to refresh my
memory. One of your colleagues suggested that I
might have gone to Pittsburgh to look at the picture. I
suppose he was being funny."

A flicker of annoyance in his fine dark eyes, which
were as clear and bright as if he had had a good eight
hours of innocent slumber, warned me that I was supposed to have read his statement, and if I aroused a
suspicion that I hadn't he might get personal.

I gave him an earnest eye. "Look, Mr. Chaffee. This
thing is bad for all concerned. It will get worse instead
of better until we find out who killed Kampf. You men
in this house must know things about one another, and
maybe some things connected with Kampf, that you're
not telling. I don't expect a man like you to pass out
dirt just for the hell of it, but any dirt that's connected
with this murder is going to come out, and if you know
of any and are keeping it to yourself you're a bigger
fool than you look."

"Quite a speech." He was smiling again.

"Thanks. You make one."

"I'm not as eloquent as you are." He shook his
head. "No, I don't believe I can help you any. I can't
say I'm a total stranger to dirt; that would be smug;

but what you're after—no. You have my opinion of Kampf, whom I knew quite well; he was in some respects admirable but had his full share of faults. I would say approximately the same of Talento. I have known Aland only casually—certainly not intimately. I know no more of Meegan than you do. I haven't the slightest notion why any of them might have wanted to kill Philip Kampf. If you expect—"

A phone rang. Chaffee crossed to a table at the end of the divan and answered it. He told it yes a couple of times, and then a few words, and then, "But one of your men is here now. . . . I don't know his name, I didn't ask him. . . . He may be, I don't know. . . . Very well, one-fifty-five Leonard Street. . . . Yes, I can leave in a few minutes."

He hung up and turned to me. I spoke first, on my feet. "So they want you at the DA's office. Don't tell them I said so, but they'd rather keep a murder in the file till hell freezes over than have the squad crack it. If they want my name they know where to ask."

I marched to the door, opened it, and was gone.

There were still no PD cars out in front. After turning left on Court Street and continuing two blocks, I was relieved to find the cab still there, with its passenger perched on the seat looking out at the scenery. If the hackie had gone off with him to sell him, or if Stebbins had happened by and hijacked him, I wouldn't have dared to go home at all. He seemed pleased to see me, as he damned well should have been. During the drive to Thirty-fifth Street he sat with his rump braced against me for a buttress. The meter said only six dollars and something, but I didn't request any change. If Wolfe wanted to put me to work on a murder merely because he had got infatuated with a dog, let it cost him something.

I noticed that when we entered the office Jet went over to Wolfe, in place behind his desk, without any sign of bashfulness or uncertainty, proving that the evening before, during my absence, Wolfe had made approaches, probably had fed him something, and possibly had even patted him. Remarks occurred to me, but I saved them. I might be called on before long to spend some valuable time demonstrating that I had not been guilty of impersonating an officer, and that it wasn't my fault if murder suspects mistook me for one.

Wolfe put down his empty beer glass and inquired, "Well?"

I reported. The situation called for a full and detailed account, and I supplied it, with Wolfe leaning back with his eyes closed. When I came to the end he asked no questions. Instead, he opened his eyes, straightened up, and began, "Call the—"

I cut him off. "Wait a minute. After a hard morning's work I claim the satisfaction of suggesting it myself. I thought of it long ago. What's the name of the Institute in Pittsburgh where they have shows of pictures?"

"Indeed. It's a shot at random."

"I know it is, but it's only a buck. I just spent ten on a taxi. What's the name?"

"Pittsburgh Art Institute."

I swiveled for the phone on my desk, got the operator, and put in the call. I got through to the Institute in no time, but it took a quarter of an hour, with relays to three different people, to get what I was after.

I hung up and turned to Wolfe. "The show ended a week ago yesterday. Thank God I won't have to go to Pittsburgh. The picture was lent by Mr. Herman Braunstein of New York, who owns it. It was shipped back to him by express four days ago. He wouldn't give me Braunstein's address."

"The phone book."

I had it and was flipping the pages. "Here we are. Business on Broad Street, residence on Park Avenue. There's only one Herman."

"Get him."

"I don't think so. He may be a poop. It might take all day. Why don't I go to the residence without phoning? It's probably there, and if I can't get in you can fire me. I'm thinking of resigning anyhow."

He had his doubts, since it was my idea, but he bought it. After considering the problem a little, I went to the cabinet beneath the bookshelves, got out the Veblex camera, with accessories, slung the strap of the case over my shoulder, told Wolfe I wouldn't be back until I saw the picture, wherever it was, and beat it. Before going I dialed Talento's number to tell him not to bother to keep his appointment, but there was no answer. Either he was still engaged at the DA's office or he was on his way to Thirty-fifth Street, and if he came during my absence that was all right, since Jet was there to protect Wolfe.

A taxi took me to the end of a sidewalk canopy in front of one of the palace hives on Park Avenue in the Seventies, and I undertook to walk past the doorman without giving him a glance, but he stopped me. I said professionally, "Braunstein, taking pictures, I'm late," and kept going, and got away with it. After crossing the luxurious lobby to the elevator, which luckily was there with the door open, I entered, saying, "Braunstein, please," and the chauffeur shut the door and pulled the lever. We stopped at the twelfth floor, and I stepped out. There was a door to the right and another to the left, and I turned right without asking, on a fifty-fifty chance, listening for a possible correction from the elevator man, who was standing by with his door open.

It was one of the simplest chores I have ever performed. In answer to my ring the door was opened by a middle-aged female husky, in uniform with apron, and when I told her I had come to take a picture she let me in, asked me to wait, and disappeared. In a couple of minutes a tall and dignified dame with white hair came through an arch and asked what I wanted. I apologized for disturbing her and said I would deeply appreciate it if she would let me take a picture of a painting which had recently been shown at the Pittsburgh Institute, on loan by Mr. Braunstein. It was called "Three Young Mares at Pasture." A Pittsburgh client of mine had admired it, and had intended to go back and photograph it for his collection, but the picture had gone before he got around to it.

She wanted some information, such as my name and address and the name of my Pittsburgh client, which I supplied gladly without a script, and then led me through the arch into a room not quite as big as Madison Square Garden. It would have been a pleasure, and also instructive, to do a little glomming at the rugs and furniture and other miscellaneous objects, especially the dozen or more pictures on the walls, but that would have to wait. She went across to a picture near the far end, said, "That's it," and lowered herself onto a chair.

It was a nice picture. I had half expected the mares to be without clothes, but they were fully dressed. Remarking that I didn't wonder that my client wanted a photograph of it, I got busy with my equipment, including flash bulbs. She sat and watched. I took four shots from slightly different angles, acting and looking professional, I hoped; got my stuff back in the case; thanked her warmly on behalf of my client; promised to send her some prints; and left. That was all there was to it.

Out on the sidewalk again, I walked west to Madison, turned downtown and found a drugstore, went in to the phone booth, and dialed a number.

Wolfe's voice came. "Yes? Whom do you want?"

I've told him a hundred times that's a hell of a way to answer the phone, but he's too damn pigheaded.

I spoke. "I want you. I've seen the picture, and I wouldn't have thought that stallion had it in him. It glows with color and life, and the blood seems to pulsate under the warm skin. The shadows are transparent, with a harmonious blending—"

"Shut up! Yes or no?"

"Yes. You have met Mrs. Meegan. Would you like to meet her again?"

"I would. Get her."

I didn't have to look in the phone book for her address, having already done so. I left the drugstore and flagged a taxi.

There was no doorman problem at the number on East Forty-ninth Street. It was an old brick house that had been painted a bright yellow and modernized, notably with a self-service elevator, though I didn't know that until I got in. Getting in was a little complicated. Pressing the button marked "Jewel Jones" in the vestibule was easy enough, and also unhooking the receiver and putting it to my ear, and placing my mouth close to the grille, but then it got more difficult.

A voice crackled. "Yes?"

"Miss Jones?"

"Yes. Who is it?"

"Archie Goodwin. I want to see you. Not a message from Victor Talento."

"What do you want?"

"Let me in and I'll tell you."

"No. What is it?"

"It's very personal. If you don't want to hear it from me I'll go and bring Richard Meegan, and maybe you'll tell him."

I heard the gasp. She should have known those house phones are sensitive. After a pause. "Why do you say that? I told you I don't know any Meegan."

"You're way behind. I just saw a picture called 'Three Young Mares at Pasture.' Let me in."

Another pause, and the line went dead. I put the receiver on the hook, and turned and placed my hand on the knob. There was a click, and I pushed the door and entered, crossed the little lobby to the elevator, pushed the button and, when the door opened, slid in, pushed the button marked 5, and was ascending. When the elevator stopped I opened the door and emerged into a tiny foyer. A door was standing open, and on the sill was Miss Jones in a blue negligee. She started to say something, but I rudely ignored it.

"Listen," I said, "There's no sense in prolonging this. Last night I gave you your pick between Mr. Wolfe and Sergeant Stebbins; now it's either Mr. Wolfe or Meegan. I should think you'd prefer Mr. Wolfe because he's the kind of man that understands; you said so yourself. I'll wait here while you change, but don't try phoning anybody, because you won't know where you are until you've talked with Mr. Wolfe, and also because their wires are probably tapped. Don't put on anything red. Mr. Wolfe dislikes red. He likes yellow."

She stepped to me and had a hand on my arm. "Archie. Where did you see the picture?"

"I'll tell you on the way down. Let's go."

She gave the arm a gentle tug. "You don't have to wait out here. Come in and sit down." Another tug, just as gentle. "Come on."

I patted her fingers, not wishing to be boorish. "Sorry," I told her, "but I'm afraid of young mares. One kicked me once."

She turned and disappeared into the apartment, leaving the door standing open.

VI

"Don't call me Mrs. Meegan!" Jewel Jones cried.

Wolfe was in as bad a humor as she was. True, she had been hopelessly cornered, with no weapons within reach, but he had been compelled to tell Fritz to postpone lunch until further notice.

"I was only," he said crustily, "stressing the fact that your identity is not a matter for discussion. Legally you are Mrs. Richard Meegan. That understood, I'll call you anything you say. Miss Jones?"

"Yes." She was on the red leather chair, but not in it. Just on its edge, she looked as if she were set to spring up and scoot any second.

"Very well." Wolfe regarded her. "You realize, madam, that everything you say will be received skeptically. You are a competent liar. Your offhand denial of acquaintance with Mr. Meegan last night was better than competent. Now. When did Mr. Chaffee tell you that your husband was in town looking for you?"

"I didn't say Mr. Chaffee told me."

"Someone did. Who and when?"

She was hanging on. "How do you know someone did?"

He wiggled a finger at her. "I beg you, Miss Jones, to realize the pickle you're in. It is not credible that Mr. Chaffee couldn't remember the name of the model for that figure in his picture. The police don't believe it, and they haven't the advantage of knowing, as I do, that it was you and that you lived in that house for a year, and that you still see Mr. Chaffee occasionally. When your husband came and asked Mr. Chaffee for the name, and Mr. Chaffee pleaded a faulty memory, and your husband rented an apartment there and made it plain that he intended to persevere, it is preposterous to suppose that Mr. Chaffee didn't tell you. I don't envy you your tussles with the police after they learn about you."

"They don't have to learn about me, do they?"

"Pfui. I'm surprised they haven't got to you already, though it's been only eighteen hours. They soon will, even if not through me. I know this is no frolic for you, here with me, but they will almost make it seem so."

She was thinking. Her brow was wrinkled and her eyes straight at Wolfe. "Do you know," she asked, "what I think would be the best thing? I don't know why I didn't think of it before. You're a detective, you're an expert at helping people in trouble, and I'm certainly in trouble. I'll pay you to help me. I could pay you a little now."

"Not now or ever, Miss Jones." Wolfe was blunt. "When did Mr. Chaffee tell you that your husband was here looking for you?"

"You won't even listen to me," she complained.

"Talk sense and I will. When?"

She edged back on the chair an inch. "You don't know my husband. He was jealous about me even before we married, and then he was worse. It got so bad

I couldn't stand it, and that was why I left him. I knew if I stayed in Pittsburgh he would find me and kill me, so I came to New York. A friend of mine had come here—I mean, just a friend. I got a job at a modeling agency and made enough to live on, and I met a lot of people. Ross Chaffee was one of them, and he wanted to use me in a picture, and I let him. Of course he paid me, but that wasn't so important, because soon after that I met Phil Kampf, and he got me a tryout at a night club, and I made it. About then I had a scare, though. A man from Pittsburgh saw me at a theater and came and spoke to me, but I told him he was wrong, that I had never been in Pittsburgh."

"That was a year ago," Wolfe muttered.

"Yes. I was a little leery about the night club, in public like that, but months went by and nothing happened, and then all of a sudden this happened. Ross Chaffee phoned me that my husband had come and asked about the picture, and I asked him for God's sake not to tell him who it was, and he promised he wouldn't. You see, you don't know my husband. I knew he was trying to find me so he could kill me."

"You've said that twice. Has he ever killed anybody?"

"I didn't say anybody; I said me. I seem to have an effect on men." She gestured for understanding. "They just go for me. And Dick— Well, I know him, that's all. I left him a year and a half ago, and he's still looking for me, and that's what he's like. When Ross told me he was here I was scared stiff. I quit working at the club because he might happen to go there and see me, and I didn't hardly leave my apartment until last night."

Wolfe nodded. "To meet Mr. Talento. What for?"

"I told you."

"Yes, but then you were merely Miss Jones. Now you are also Mrs. Meegan. What for?"

"That doesn't change it any. I had heard on the radio about Phil being killed, and I wanted to know about it. I rang Ross Chaffee and I rang Jerry Aland, but neither of them answered, so I rang Vic Talento. He wouldn't tell me anything on the phone, but he said he would meet me."

"Did Mr. Aland and Mr. Talento know you had sat for that picture?"

"Sure they did."

"And that Mr. Meegan had seen it and recognized you, and was here looking for you?"

"Yes, they knew all about it. Ross had to tell them, because he thought Dick might ask them if they knew who had modeled for the picture, and he had to warn them not to tell. They said they wouldn't, and they didn't. They're all good friends of mine."

She stopped to do something. She opened her black leather bag on her lap, took out a purse, and fingered its contents, peering into it. She raised her eyes to Wolfe. "I can pay you forty dollars now, to start. I'm not just in trouble, I'm in danger of my life, really I am. I don't see how you can refuse— You're not listening!"

Apparently he wasn't. With his lips pursed, he was watching the tip of his forefinger make little circles on his desk blotter. Her reproach didn't stop him, but after a moment he moved his eyes to me and said abruptly, "Get Mr. Chaffee."

"No!" she cried. "I don't want him to know—"

"Nonsense," he snapped at her. "Everybody will have to know everything, and why drag it out? Get him, Archie. I'll speak to him."

I got at the phone and dialed. I doubted if he would be back from his session with the DA, but he was. His "hello" was enough to recognize his voice by. I pitched mine low so he wouldn't know it, not caring to start a debate as to whether I had or had not impersonated an officer, and merely told him that Nero Wolfe wished to speak to him.

Wolfe took it at his desk. "Mr. Chaffee? This is Nero Wolfe. . . . I've assumed an interest in the murder of Philip Kampf and have done some investigating. . . . Just one moment, please, don't ring off. . . . Sitting here in my office is Mrs. Richard Meegan, alias Miss Jewel Jones. . . . Please let me finish. . . . I shall of course have to detain her and communicate with the police, since they will want her as a material witness in a murder case, but before I do that I would like to discuss the matter with you and the others who live in that house. Will you undertake to bring them here as soon as possible? . . . No, I'll say nothing further on the phone, I want you here, all of you. If Mr. Meegan is balky, you might as well tell him his wife is here. I'll expect—"

She was across to him in a leap that any young mare might have envied, grabbing for the phone and shrieking at it, "Don't tell him, Ross! Don't bring him! Don't—"

My own leap and dash around the end of the desk was fairly good too. Getting her shoulders, I yanked her back, with enough enthusiasm so that I landed in the red leather chair with her on my lap, and since she was by no means through I wrapped my arms around her, pinning her arms to her sides, whereupon she started kicking my shins with her heels. She kept on kicking until Wolfe finished with Chaffee. When he hung up she suddenly relaxed and was limp, and I realized how warm she felt tight against me.

Wolfe scowled at us. "An affecting sight," he snorted.

VII

There were various aspects of the situation. One was lunch. For Wolfe it was unthinkable to have company in the house at mealtime, no matter what his or her status was, without feeding him or her, but he certainly wasn't going to sit at table with a female who had just pounced on him and clawed at him. That problem was simple. She and I were served in the dining room, and Wolfe ate in the kitchen with Fritz. We were served, but she didn't eat much. She kept listening and looking toward the hall, though I assured her that care would be taken to see that her husband didn't kill her on those premises.

A second aspect was the reaction of three of the tenants to their discovery of my identity. I handled that myself. When the doorbell rang and I admitted them, at a quarter past two, I told them I would be glad to discuss my split personality with any or all of them later, if they still wanted to, but they would have to file it until Wolfe was through. Victor Talento had another beef that he wouldn't file, that I had double-crossed him on the message he had asked me to take to Jewel Jones. He wanted to get nasty about it and demanded a private talk with Wolfe, but I told him to go climb a rope.

I also had to handle the third aspect, which had two angles. There was Miss Jones's theory that her husband would kill her on sight, which might or might not be well founded, and there was the fact that one of them had killed Kampf and might go to extremes if pushed. On that I took three precautions: I showed them the Carley .38 I had put in my pocket and told them it was loaded; I insisted on patting them from shoulders to ankles; and I kept Miss Jones in the dining room until I had them seated in the office, on a row of chairs facing Wolfe's desk, and until Wolfe had come in from the kitchen and been told their names. When he was in his chair behind his desk I went across the hall for her and brought her in.

Meegan jumped up and started for us. I stiff-armed him and made it good. She got behind me. Talento and Aland left their chairs, presumably to help protect the mare. Meegan was talking, and so were they. I detoured with her around back of them and got her to a chair at the end of my desk, and when I sat I was in an ideal spot to trip anyone headed for her. Talento and Aland had pulled Meegan down onto a chair between them, and he sat staring at her.

"With that hubbub over," Wolfe said, "I want to be sure I have the names right." His eyes went from left to right. "Talento, Meegan, Aland, Chaffee. Is that correct?

I told him yes.

"Then I'll proceed." He glanced up at the wall clock. "Twenty hours ago Philip Kampf was killed in the house where you gentlemen live. The circumstances indicate that one of you killed him. But I won't rehash the multifarious details which you have already discussed at length with the police; you are familiar with them. I have not been hired to work on this case; the only client I have is a dog, and he came to my office by inadvertence. However, it is—"

The doorbell rang. I asked myself if I had put the chain bolt on, and decided I had. Through the open door to the hall I saw Fritz passing to answer it. Wolfe started to go on, but was annoyed by the sound of voices, Fritz's and another's, coming through, and stopped. The voices continued. Wolfe shut his eyes and compressed his lips. The audience sat and looked at him.

Then Fritz appeared in the doorway and announced, "Inspector Cramer, sir."

Wolfe's eyes opened. "What does he want?"

"I told him you are engaged. He says he knows you are, that the four men were followed to your house and he was notified. He says he expected you to be trying some trick with the dog, and he knows that's what you are doing, and he intends to come in and see what it is. Sergeant Stebbins is with him."

Wolfe grunted. "Archie, tell—No. You'd better stay where you are. Fritz, tell him he may see and hear what I'm doing, provided he gives me thirty minutes without interruptions or demands. If he agrees to that, bring them in."

"Wait!" Ross Chaffee was on his feet. "You said you would discuss it with us before you communicated with the police."

"I haven't communicated with them, they're here."

"You told them to come!"

"No. I would have preferred to deal with you men first and then call them, but here they are and they might as well join us. Bring them, Fritz, on that condition."

"Yes, sir."

Fritz went. Chaffee thought he had something more to say, decided he hadn't, and sat down. Talento said something to him, and he shook his head. Jerry Aland, much more presentable now that he was combed and dressed, kept his eyes fastened on Wolfe.

For Meegan, apparently, there was no one in the room but him and his wife.

Cramer and Stebbins marched in, halted three paces from the door, and took a survey.

"Be seated," Wolfe invited them. "Luckily, Mr. Cramer, your usual chair is unoccupied."

"Where's the dog?" Cramer barked.

"In the kitchen. You had better suspend that prepossession. It's understood that you will be merely a spectator for thirty minutes?"

"That's what I said."

"Then sit down. But you should have one piece of information. You know the gentlemen, of course, but not the lady. Her current name is Miss Jewel Jones. Her legal name is Mrs. Richard Meegan."

"Meegan?" Cramer stared. "The one in the picture Chaffee painted? Meegan's wife?"

"That's right. Please be seated."

"Where did you get her?"

"That can wait. No interruptions and no demands. Confound it, sit down!"

Cramer went and lowered himself onto the red leather chair. Purley Stebbins got one of the yellow ones and planted it behind the row, between Chaffee and Aland.

Wolfe regarded the quartet. "I was about to say, gentlemen, that it was something the dog did that pointed to the murderer for me. But before—"

"What did it do?" Cramer barked.

"You know all about it," Wolfe told him coldly. "Mr. Goodwin related it to you exactly as it happened. If you interrupt again, by heaven, you can take them all down to your quarters, not including the dog, and stew it out yourself."

He went back to the four. "But before I come to

that, another thing or two. I offer no comment on your guile with Mr. Meegan. You were all friends of Miss Jones's, having, I suppose, enjoyed various degrees of intimacy with her, and you refused to disclose her to a husband whom she had abandoned and professed to fear. I will even concede that there was a flavor of gallantry in your conduct. But when Mr. Kampf was murdered and the police swarmed in, it was idiotic to try to keep her out of it. They were sure to get to her. I got to her first only because of Mr. Goodwin's admirable enterprise and characteristic luck."

He shook his head at them. "It was also idiotic of you to assume that Mr. Goodwin was a police officer, and admit him and answer his questions, merely because he had been present during the abortive experiment with the dog. You should have asked to see his credentials. None of you had any idea who he was. Even Mr. Meegan, who had seen him in this office in the morning, was bamboozled. I mention this to anticipate any possible official complaint that Mr. Goodwin impersonated an officer. You know he didn't. He merely took advantage of your unwarranted assumption."

He shifted in his chair. "Another thing. Yesterday morning Mr. Meegan called here by appointment to ask me to do a job for him. With his first words I gathered that it was something about his wife, and I don't take that kind of work, and I was brusque with him. He was offended. He rushed out in a temper, getting his hat and raincoat from the rack in the hall, and he took Mr. Goodwin's coat instead of his own. Late in the afternoon Mr. Goodwin went to Arbor Street, with the coat that had been left in error, to exchange it. He saw that in front of number twenty-nine there were collected two police cars, a policeman on post, some peo-

ple, and a dog. He decided to postpone his errand and
went on by, after a brief halt during which he patted
the dog. He walked home, and had gone nearly two
miles when he discovered that the dog was following
him. He brought the dog in a cab the rest of the way,
to this house and this room."

He flattened a palm on his desk. "Now. Why did the
dog follow Mr. Goodwin through the turmoil of the
city? Mr. Cramer's notion that the dog was enticed is
poppycock. Mr. Goodwin is willing to believe, as many
men are, that he is irresistible to both dogs and
women, and doubtless his vanity impeded his intellect
or he would have reached the same conclusion that I
did. The dog didn't follow him; it followed the coat. You
ask, as I did, how to account for Mr. Kampf's dog following Mr. Meegan's coat. I couldn't. I can't. Then,
since it was unquestionably Mr. Kampf's dog, it
couldn't have been Mr. Meegan's coat. It is better than
a conjecture, it is next thing to a certainty, that it was
Mr. Kampf's coat."

His gaze leveled at the husband. "Mr. Meegan.
Some two hours ago I learned from Mr. Goodwin that
you maintain that you had never seen or heard of Mr.
Kampf. That was fairly conclusive, but before sending
for you I had to verify my conjecture that the model
who had sat for Mr. Chaffee's picture was your wife. I
would like to hear it straight from you. Did you ever
meet with Philip Kampf alive?"

Meegan was meeting the gaze. "No."

"Don't you want to qualify that?"

"No."

"Then where did you get his raincoat?"

No answer. Meegan's jaw worked. He spoke. "I
didn't have his raincoat, or if I did I didn't know it."

"That won't do. I warn you, you are in deadly peril.

The raincoat that you brought into this house and left here is in the hall now, there on the rack. It can easily be established that it belonged to Mr. Kampf and was worn by him. Where did you get it?"

Meegan's jaw worked some more. "I never had it, if it belonged to Kampf. This is a dirty frame. You can't prove that's the coat I left here."

Wolfe's voice sharpened. "One more chance. Have you any explanation of how Kampf's coat came into your possession?"

"No, and I don't need any."

He may not have been pure boob. If he hadn't noticed that he wore the wrong coat home, and he probably didn't, in his state of mind, this had hit him from a clear sky and he had no time to study it.

"Then you're done for," Wolfe told him. "For your own coat must be somewhere, and I think I know where. In the police laboratory. Mr. Kampf was wearing one when you killed him and pushed his body down the stairs—and that explains why, when they were making that experiment this morning, the dog showed no interest in the spot where the body had lain. It had been enveloped, not in his coat but in yours. That can be established too. If you won't explain how you got Mr. Kampf's coat, then explain how he got yours. Is that also a frame?"

Wolfe pointed a finger at him. "I note that flash in your eye, and I think I know what it means. But your brain is lagging. If, after killing him, you took your raincoat off of him and put on him the one that you thought was his, that won't help you any. For in that case the coat that was on the body is Mr. Goodwin's, and certainly that can be established, and how would you explain that? It looks hopeless, and—"

Meegan was springing up, but before he even got

well started Purley's big hands were on his shoulders, pulling him back and down. And a new voice sounded.

"I told you he would kill me! I knew he would! He killed Phil!"

Jewel Jones was looking not at her husband, who was under control, but at Wolfe. He snapped at her, "How do you know he did?"

Judging by her eyes and the way she was shaking, she would be hysterical in another two minutes, and maybe she knew it, for she poured it out. "Because Phil told me—he told me he knew Dick was here looking for me, and he knew how afraid I was of him, and he said if I wouldn't come and be with him again he would tell Dick where I was. I didn't think he really would—I didn't think Phil could be as mean as that, and I wouldn't promise, but yesterday morning he phoned me and told me he had seen Dick and told him he thought he knew who had posed for that picture, and he was going to see him again in the afternoon and tell him about me if I didn't promise, and so I promised. I thought if I promised it would give me time to decide what to do. But Phil must have gone to see Dick again anyway—"

"Where had they met in the morning?"

"At Phil's apartment, he said. And he said—that's why I know Dick killed him—he said Dick had gone off with his raincoat, and he laughed about it and said he was willing for Dick to have his raincoat if he could have Dick's wife." She was shaking harder now. "And I'll bet that's what he told Dick! That was like Phil! I'll bet he told Dick I was coming back to him and he thought that was a good trade, a raincoat for a wife! That was like Phil! You don't—"

She giggled. It started with a giggle, and then the valves busted open and here it came. When something happens in that office to smash a woman's nerves, as it has more than once, it usually falls to me to deal with it, but that time three other guys, led by Ross Chaffee, came to her, and I was glad to leave it to them. As for Wolfe, he skedaddled. If there is one thing on earth he absolutely will not be in a room with it's a woman in eruption. He got up and marched out. As for Meegan, Purley and Cramer had him.

When they left with him, they didn't take the dog. To relieve the minds of any of you who have the notion, which I understand is widespread, that it makes a dog neurotic to change its name, I might add that he responds to Jet now as if his mother had started calling him that before he had his eyes open.

As for the raincoat, Wolfe had been right about the flash in Meegan's eye. Kampf had been wearing Meegan's raincoat when he was killed, and of course that wouldn't do, so after strangling him Meegan had taken it off and put on the one he thought was Kampf's. Only it was mine. As a part of the DA's case I went down to headquarters and identified it. At the trial it helped the jury to decide that Meegan deserved the big one. After that was over I suppose I could have claimed it, but the idea didn't appeal to me. My new one is a different color.

The World of Rex Stout

Now, for the first time ever, enjoy a peek into the life of Nero Wolfe's creator, Rex Stout, courtesy of the Stout Estate. Pulled from Rex Stout's own archives, here are rarely seen, never-before-published memorabilia. Each title in "The Rex Stout Library" will offer an exclusive look into the life of the man who gave Nero Wolfe life.

Three Witnesses

In 1967 Rex Stout was approached by the school newspaper of Junior High School 115 in New York City and asked the following question: "Which book or books were your favorites as a teenager and why?" Stout's reply is reproduced here.

I was an insatiable book reader from the age of five. The list below of some of my favorites as a teenager may give the impression that I am showing off, but I'm not: it is quite honest.

History _of_ _England_ by Macaulay, _Essays_ by Francis Bacon, _Alice_ _in_ _Wonderland_ by Lewis Carroll, _Vanity_ _Fair_ by Thackeray, _Little_ _Lord_ _Fauntleroy_ by Frances Hodgson Burnett, _Les_ _Miserables_ by Victor Hugo, _Poems_ by John Keats, _Paradise_ _Lost_ by John Milton, the Sherlock Holmes stories by Conan Doyle, _Little_ _Women_ by Louisa May Alcott, _Tom_ _Sawyer_ by Mark Twain, and the novels and stories of Rudyard Kipling.

Thank you for reminding me of those wonderful days when I read so many exciting things the first time.

Sincerely,

Rex Stout